COLD JADE

JOHN ROCKNE MYSTERY #3

DAN AMES

COLD JADE

(A John Rockne Mystery)

by

Dan Ames

FOREWORD

Do you want more killer crime fiction, along with the chance to win free books? Then join:
THE DAN AMES BOOK CLUB

Go to AuthorDanAmes.com

PRAISE FOR THE JOHN ROCKNE
MYSTERY SERIES

Dan Ames' writing reminds me of the great thriller writers -- lean, mean, no nonsense prose that gets straight to the point and keeps you turning those pages."

–author Robert Gregory Browne

"As gritty as the Detroit streets where it's set, DEAD WOOD grabs you early on and doesn't let go. As fine a a debut as you'll come across this year, maybe any year."

-author Tom Schreck

"From its opening lines, Daniel S. Ames and his private eye novel DEAD WOOD recall early James Ellroy: a fresh attitude and voice and the heady rush of boundless yearning and ambition. Ames delivers a vivid evocation of time and place in a way that few debut authors achieve, nailing the essence of his chosen corner of high-tone Michigan. He also deftly dodges the pitfalls that make so much contemporary private detective fiction a mixed bag and nostalgia-freighted misfire. Ames' detective has family; he's steady. He's not another burned-out, booze-hound hanging on teeth and toenails to the world and smugly wallowing in his own ennui. This is the first new private eye novel in a long time that just swept me along for the ride. Ames is definitely one to watch."

-*Craig McDonald, Edgar-nominated author*

"Dead Wood is a fast-paced, unpredictable mystery with an engaging narrator and a rich cast of original supporting characters."

-*New York Times bestselling author Thomas Perry*

"In DEAD WOOD, Dan Ames pulls off a very difficult thing: he re-imagines what a hardboiled mystery can be, and does it with style, thrills and humor. This is the kind of book mystery readers are clamoring for, a fast-paced story with great heart and not a cliché to be found. DEAD WOOD is a hell of a book."

–*Amazon.com*

"Dan Ames is a sensation among readers who love fast-paced thrillers."

–*Mystery Tribune*

"A smart detective story stuffed with sharp prose and snappy one liners."

–*Indie Reader*

"Packed to the gills with hard-hitting action and a non-stop plot."

-Jacksonville News

"Cuts like a knife."

-Savannah Morning News

THE SERIES FROM THE BEGINNING

COLD JADE

John Rockne Mystery #3

by

Dan Ames

"It is double pleasure to deceive the deceiver."
-Niccolo Machiavelli

She weighed a hundred pounds soaking wet but could put away tequila like a Colombian foot soldier just back from three months in the jungle. How many had she thrown back? Five? Six?

Either way, the tingling in her hands, the numbness along her jaw was kind of new.

That part of it could be the drugs.

Around her, people swirled in a cloud of perfume and bright clothes, bounced to and from by a pulsating bass beat that seemed to hit her from every direction, like she was running an invisible gauntlet.

An even more intense wave of disorientation hit her, she knew it wasn't from the booze. And probably not from the drugs she took, even though she couldn't remember what the pills had been or who had given them to her.

Maybe I've been roofied, she thought. And then she started laughing.

The problem was the friend she'd been with was now gone. But damn, she couldn't remember his name. Or was it a her? Everything seemed confusing, especially when her breath caught and somewhere there was a crashing bang followed by the unmistakable sound of breaking glass.

She looked down and saw a champagne glass at her feet, or at least what was left of it.

Several sets of eyes loomed before her, one person's mouth formed into a perfect "O" as she struggled to walk past. Ahead, the front door to the huge house looked like a gateway to a different world. And that's where she wanted to go. A world. That was different.

The front door tilted as she approached it, wobbling on her stiletto heels, and she leaned to the side, because the door was crooked and she had to try to make it through. Instead, her head hit the door frame and it made a solid thunking sound but she felt no pain. The blow to her head pushed her upright and she made it all the way through the door, pushing the dark, heavy wood forcing it to surrender to her shoulder.

It swung all the way open, then bounced off its backstop before swinging back and slamming shut.

The silence and darkness hit her like a splash of cold water.

Her eyes finally opened all the way and she moved forward, not realizing there was a step from the wide front porch down to the walk.

Her leg buckled and her momentum carried her forward. She took a faltering step but she was already leaning too far forward and her legs couldn't catch up.

She landed face first in the wet grass.

Her nose must have hit first because there was a tiny shadow of pain that crossed her eyes and then she tasted something in her mouth. Something that wasn't water from the grass, but a thick liquid with a metallic flavor.

"Mmm, this blood is delicious," she slurred.

With a monumental effort she turned herself onto her back. The sky was now a blanket of black with holes poked in it by distant stars.

She knew she needed to get up, call someone. Maybe Lace. Or AJ. But not her Mom or Dad. Hell, no. She planned on never talking to either of them again for the rest of her life.

The hope had been to make tonight a nice score, but things had clearly gotten out of hand.

She giggled again. Tried to stand up.

But she couldn't move.

She could only blink.

And smell the grass.

Taste a droplet of water, mixed with blood, on her tongue.

And watch as a dark figure circled around her.

She wanted to ask for help, but her mouth couldn't move. No words came out, only a gasp and a sputter.

The shadow stopped. A pair of men's shoes, brown leather, came to a stop inches from her face.

She heard a voice speak.

"I thought yesterday was trash day," it said.

One of the shoes was lifted out of her vision.

When it smashed back down, she felt nothing.

W e met at a bar on Mack Avenue. It was a dark, dingy kind of place where if you had to eat, you chose the burger as it would be the only safe option. Not exactly the ideal restaurant to order a Nicoise salad.

Marvin Cotton was a short, stocky black man with big round eyes and heavy cheeks. He had just a brush of gray at his temples.

He had called me earlier in the day and requested a meeting, preferably not in Grosse Pointe. The bar I'd suggested was a few blocks over the border into Detroit. It was called The Peg.

I guessed who my potential client was and approached him.

"Mr. Cotton?" I said.

He was half-turned toward the door, a draft beer on the bar in front of him. He stuck out his hand.

"Mr. Rockne?" he said.

We shook and I slid onto the bar stool next to him.

"Thanks for meeting me," he said.

"Thank you for giving me a call," I said. I ordered a draft of a beer called Dirty Blonde. Who didn't mind a dirty blonde now and then?

"How'd you find me by the way?" I asked. It was always interesting, and a good business practice to find out where your referrals were coming from.

Mr. Cotton mentioned a former client of mine who'd been wrongly fired for being a whistleblower. With the help of an attorney and the evidence of wrongdoing that confirmed his claims, we ultimately got him a very nice settlement.

"You're probably wondering why I didn't want to meet in Grosse Pointe," he said.

I shook my head. "Not my place to wonder, or question. I get paid to be curious about what my clients want me to be questioning. That's what I focus on."

Besides, future clients always requested somewhere unusual to meet. Someplace they considered out of the way. No matter how big a community, there's always a chance of bumping into someone. I was in Chicago once and bumped into an old girlfriend. I don't think she remembered me, which was kind of par for the course.

"Honestly, I wanted to meet here because my wife doesn't really want me to be doing this," Marvin said. "She didn't want me to hire anyone. Said to let the police do their job. Plus, she's frugal as hell and would kill me if she knew I was here. Talking to a private investigator."

I nodded, took a sip of my Dirty Blonde. It was good. Smooth. All my life I've been attracted to brunettes. You never know what the day is going to bring.

"So you said the police are involved. What's going on?"

"It's our daughter," he said. His face seemed to collapse around itself. His mouth sagged, shoulders slumped. If ever the phrase 'the life seemed to go out of him' applied to someone, it applied to Marvin Cotton.

"Kierra. Kierra Cotton," he said. "My baby girl. She's been missing for nearly three weeks and the cops don't have jack."

"How old is Kierra?"

"She's eighteen."

I nodded and then took out my notebook and pen.

"When did you see her last?"

Marvin sighed. "The scene of the granddaddy Cotton family fight of all time," he said. "My wife and Kierra really got into it. Screaming. Name calling. Kierra stormed out and we haven't seen or heard from her since."

In the back, someone fired up the juke box with a country song about buying a boat.

"So do you think she ran away?" I said. I'd seen it a million times. Big fight, kid runs away to 'get even' with the parents. Sometimes, they come crawling back after a few days not liking the big, bad world without the safety blanket of Mom and Dad. Sometimes, rarely, they decide they like the big, bad world a whole lot more on their own.

He shook his head. "Initially I think she just wanted some space. But then I think something happened. We've had fights before. Some pretty big disagreements. But Kierra and I are very close. She's always been my girl."

Marvin's face cracked a little bit and he took a sip of his beer.

"She would have let me know after a day or two that everything was fine and where she was," he added.

That one did give me pause, I have to admit. When someone breaks a familiar pattern or behaves in a way that people close to them call it unusual, it can be a sign of something more serious underfoot.

"Have you tried to locate her cell phone?" I asked.

He nodded. "It doesn't show up anywhere. She didn't use it once after the argument."

"Did the police say they're checking with your carrier?"

"Yes, they said that, but we haven't heard if they've found anything. I logged onto our account and looked for activity, but it stopped the day we last heard from her."

"What about her email and social media accounts?" I asked. "Did she have her own computer at home that she was still logged into?"

"No, she wanted a laptop but we couldn't swing it. Besides, these phones nowadays are practically computers anyway. We told her if she went to college we would get her one."

His voice caught on the 'if she went to college' line and he took another drink of his beer, this one longer.

"Was she planning on going to college?" I said.

"She had the grades to go. She took the ACT and did great. She even applied to some schools at the beginning of her senior year but then…"

He shrugged his shoulders.

I knew there was a lot more to the story, but I didn't want to press him.

"Can you help?" he asked, after draining the last of his beer.

"I can," I said. "What I can't do is make any promises. If she's truly dropped off the grid, it will be difficult. But nothing is impossible. Sometimes I've found people her age in a couple of hours. Some of them have taken longer." I left out the part about a few never being found.

We sat in silence for a few moments.

"Do you have daughters?" he asked me.

"Two."

That seemed to help him make up his mind.

"Tell me what you need to get started," he said.

The abandoned factory sat along Jefferson Avenue, a huge, hulking structure that looked like an abandoned set from a science fiction movie. It went on for several city blocks and Clay Hitchfield immediately began to think of breaking in, what might be worth stealing, what kind of security would be present, and if it would be worth a trip back to the slammer.

Considering that he'd just gotten out, and narrowly avoided going right back in thanks to the partner he was about to meet, he decided it wasn't. Besides, Detroit was a rat's nest. Every abandoned building in the city had been pretty much picked clean. Most of the time all you found inside were a bunch of junkies with rusty switchblades and toothless gums.

He cruised past the factory in his twenty-year-old Dodge Ram pickup he'd bought with the first of the cash, until he came to the park that butted up against the abandoned property.

Weird place for a park, he thought. But it was a park,

even though the benches were covered with bird shit and there were more weeds than grass.

Clay pulled into the parking lot, and noted there were no other vehicles around. Across the street from the park was a collection of stores that had seen better days, too. A drug store, a liquor store, and a shuttered grocery store.

He saw the man in the suit sitting on one of the grimy park benches, probably worried about his clothes.

He parked across the street so I couldn't see his car.

Clay knew how these things worked. Sure, there'd been a couple trips to prison, but those had not been his fault. He'd simply worked with a bunch of dumbasses. And maybe his anger had gotten out of control a few times, but it wasn't his fault. There were just so many scumbags in the world whose stupidity sometimes got the best of him.

The big Ram truck barely fit into the space he chose. They must have painted the lines of the parking lot and assumed everyone drove some little rice burner piece of shit Toyota.

Last time he checked, he was still in America, goddamnit.

The man on the bench was looking at his phone and didn't bother to raise his head when Clay shut off the big truck's engine. Although Clay thought he saw the man's eyes glance over and then make a quick scan of the area.

Nervous.

Clay smiled, got out of the truck and walked up to the bench.

"Hello, Clay," the man said. He had a deep voice, clear blue eyes, and wavy gray hair. He was also a big dude, Clay could see that even though he was sitting down. The guy reminded him of an old movie star. From a couple of westerns. The guy that kind of walked funny.

John Wayne. Yeah, that was the actor. John fucking Wayne. Big as life.

"Hey," Clay said and stayed standing. He knew they made an odd couple, this big guy, dressed in the nice suit with the silver hair, looking like he could clear a town of outlaws all by himself. And then he, Clay Hitchfield, not even six feet tall and weighing no more than a hundred and fifty pounds soaking wet, with tattoos all over his arms, a shaved head, neck tattoos and a pair of jeans and a T-shirt, neither of which had been washed since he'd gotten out of lockup.

"Thanks for meeting me," the man said. His voice was deep and powerful, but his tone didn't seem thankful at all.

Clay had a few questions of his own, but he saw a slight bulge in the man's suit jacket and he hoped it wasn't a gun. That would be bad news for the man, since the knife in the waistband of Clay's jeans would be out quicker than you could say boo and would make an awful mess of the man's throat. What he really hoped is that the bulge was a bit of money, since Clay never did jobs without a steady payment system of cash. So he kept the questions to himself and let the man speak.

"We need you to find someone," the man said. He leaned over and Clay saw a couple sheets of paper, two photographs and a cell phone.

The man handed it all to Clay.

"Her name is Kierra Cotton, but everyone calls her Jade. She's missing. And this is the man who probably knows where she is." The man pointed at a photograph of a young black man. Clay's stomach turned at the sight of the black punk giving the camera a tough-guy stare and a sideways peace sign. *What the hell did that mean anyway?*

"His name is AJ," the man continued. "There's a little

information in there about him, address and such, but you'll need to find more. He's a drug dealer."

"Of course he is, that's what they do," Clay said.

"Who?" the man asked.

"The blacks. That's what they do. Sell drugs. Have babies. Go on welfare."

Clay took the photographs and looked at them more closely. The woman was sort of pretty for her kind. The guy looked like your typical ghetto scum.

"The phone is a burner, already loaded with minutes and my phone number," the man said.

The man's voice changed register just a hair, and Clay smiled inside. It wasn't really his phone number. It was just a number for another burner phone. More attempts to distance himself from Clay, it was why he parked across the street in the mall.

"In the envelope is two thousand dollars cash. When you find her and either bring her to me, or bring me to her, I'll give you eight thousand more."

Ten grand. Clay could use ten grand right about now. He thought about asking for more, but since this was his first job with this big dude, he'd take the first offer. Once they were further into the shit together, Clay knew he would have some leverage. This was the kind of guy that cared a lot about appearances. And he'd pay to keep that image as clean as possible.

"There are quite a few very important people involved in this," the man said. "Dangerous people. If you do anything other than what I'm asking you to do, you'll probably disappear, too. The only difference is no one will ever look for you."

"You making a threat?" Clay said. He smiled, but prison had taught him to always strike first. At the first sign of trouble. And he was satisfied to see a flicker of fear in the man's eyes.

"Just letting you know the situation," the man said, clearing his throat. He lifted his chin toward Clay's truck. "I'll let you leave first. Call me as soon as you find something out. And don't call me until you do."

Clay hesitated just long enough to let the man know he wasn't some trained monkey, and then walked back to the truck and fired it up. He wasn't going to hang around anyway. And he certainly wasn't going to follow the man. Hell, a quick glance at the mall parking lot and he'd spotted the big black BMW parked on the opposite end right away.

No need to push it. For now.

There'd be plenty of time for him to find out exactly who John Wayne was. And if there was more money for him than just the ten grand.

Clay had a feeling there was more.

A lot more.

Facebook.

Twitter.

Instagram.

Snapchat.

"Jesus, doesn't anyone talk to each other anymore?" I asked my wife.

We were sitting together on the couch, Anna had a Kindle in her hand, I had the iPad. The girls (we have two) were upstairs in bed.

"I'm sorry, what did you say?" she said with a smirk on her face. Anna kidded around just as much as I did, if not more. "Something about talking?"

I was looking over the email Marvin Cotton had sent me, that included some of Kierra's usernames on social media. Unfortunately, he didn't have any of her passwords. Instead, he'd sent me the names of her pets, their street address, her birthdate, anything that might help me guess her passwords.

I didn't have much hope.

"Look at these websites," I said. "Instead of people actually talking. And it's all fake. No one ever posts a shot of them sitting home alone with a box of Twinkies and a bottle of schnapps."

"You mean no photos of you when you were single?" my wife said. Smarty pants.

"It's so sad," I continued, ignoring her, even though she was half right. About the Twinkies, not the schnapps. I hated schnapps.

"The best parts of my childhood were hanging out with my buddies in the middle of nowhere," I said. "Riding bikes in the hills. Long walks. Swimming at the dead-end street that ran directly into the lake. All of that would have been ruined with cell phones."

"It's funny, though," my wife said. "Everything is documented. These kids have pictures of everything and they're stored forever as they're digital." She leaned back and looked up at the ceiling. "Seriously, I probably have like five or six pictures of me with my best friend from grade school."

"That's true, but are our daughters going to know how to live in the moment? Or are they going to be constantly distracted by these stupid things?" I asked, holding up my iPhone.

"Oh, you love being on Twitter. Don't act like you don't."

It was true. I didn't mind Twitter. Or Facebook. But I really only used them to market my private investigator services. My Facebook page was up to two hundred Likes. But I had to learn how to use all of the social media outlets. Instagram? Tumblr? As a professional, I really need to know the ins and outs of social media for cases just like Kierra Cotton's.

"I'm only on there to keep tabs on you," I said. "Make sure you're not chatting with your old boyfriends from high school."

She smiled at me. "Nice try. Besides, I blocked you. You have no idea what I'm doing online."

Anna's expression changed. "So what do you think happened to this girl?"

"No way of knowing, yet," I said. "Most of the time, it's not criminal. Staying with a friend, punishing the parents by not contacting them, that sort of thing. Kind of like the silent treatment you use on me all the time."

She smiled at me and said nothing.

"I just hope she didn't get mixed up with the wrong people," I said.

"Like gangs?"

I nodded. "Yep, recruiters. Get these girls into gangs and then take them out of state, make them totally dependent. I hope that' s not the case."

"Find her as soon as you can," she said.

I knew she was thinking about our two girls sound asleep upstairs, and what kinds of things they'd find out in the real world when they got older.

"That's the plan," I said, trying to sound as hopeful as possible.

The next morning I was at my office bright and early. Except it wasn't very bright. Michigan can be just as gloomy as the Pacific Northwest, sandwiched as it is between a few Great Lakes. And, to be honest, it wasn't all that early, either. But I do like that expression.

I fired up my computer and pulled the paperwork Marvin Cotton had given me. It included a lot of information about Kierra, hopefully that I could use to crack some of her social media accounts. If I couldn't do it, well, I had someone who could hack their way in. But I didn't want to spend the money and technically it wasn't legal. So I thought I would give it the old Rockne try first.

From what I'd heard, the kids these days were done with Facebook. Apparently, the adults had moved in and it was no longer anywhere near being cool. Supposedly, Twitter had become the next hot thing but then that had faded and now the big site was Instagram. And if you were female, Pinterest. There was also something I'd heard called Snapchat but I had no idea what the hell that was. I was pacing myself with these things, hoping that some of them would fall by the wayside and I wouldn't have to waste time learning them.

Marvin Cotton had given me a sheet of paper with most of Kierra's usernames and one password, which was for Facebook. He had explained to me that the one condition they'd insisted upon was for Kierra to give them her password when she first got Facebook.

That had been many years ago. I had very little hope that she hadn't changed her password since then.

I typed in the information and it went to her profile page.

Excellent. She hadn't changed it.

A quick glance at her profile page and I was immediately disappointed. The last post was from nearly two years ago. Apparently she had gotten the news, two years ago, that Facebook was no longer cool.

I took a quick look at the most recent pictures she had posted anyway. She was a beautiful girl. I had no way of knowing if anything from two years ago would be valuable.

Nonetheless, I dragged the photos onto my desktop and printed them off. You never knew what witnesses I might find and how long ago they had last seen her.

Just in case I bookmarked her profile and then tried the same password with her Twitter handle.

That she had changed.

And her profile was locked.

The Facebook password had been preciousbaby, named after the Cottons' miniature poodle. So I tried variations. Preciousthing. Precious. Precious followed by their address number. Preciousgirl.

Preciousgirl did the trick.

Another disappointment. She hadn't tweeted in nearly a

year. But I did notice that the last tweet was about her getting an Instagram account.

So I bookmarked her Twitter, then opened up Instagram, typed in her username and tried preciousgirl.

Bingo.

I was in.

And this time I felt a small surge of adrenaline when I saw that this page was current.

The first image I saw was of Kierra, looking a lot different than she'd looked on her two-year-old Facebook page.

That Kierra had been beautiful and youthful-looking in a healthy way.

This Kierra looked much thinner. With an edge.

In the first photo, she was holding a champagne bottle and wearing a skimpy top. Her brown skin was shiny with sweat and the muscles in her neck were visible.

She looked like she had been partying hard. For awhile.

In the images that followed she was frequently in the arms of a young man. He was tall and slim, with a snapback Detroit Tigers baseball cap and a gold chain. I read one of the captions.

"Me and AJ poppin' bottles."

Hmm.

I printed off that picture and added it to my growing collection.

Most of the images were party pictures, along with a few selfies in bathroom mirrors.

I managed to find a couple recent pictures of Kierra with two female friends who appeared in the images more than once.

With a scanner app on my phone, I scanned the image

of Kierra with AJ and texted the image to Marvin Cotton and asked him if he knew who the young man was.

I scanned in the other photos, too.

My phone buzzed and I checked the screen.

It was a text from Marvin.

Antoine James, it read. Somewhere on Lakepointe in the Park.

That was Lakepointe Avenue in Grosse Pointe Park.

Not too far from me.

Well, I had his photo and that section was only a few blocks. I figured I could ask around and find him.

It would also give me a chance to swing by the police station and find out who was handling Kierra's case.

I sort of had a source in the police department.

L ocated on Jefferson Avenue between the library and St. Ambrose Catholic Church and within a stone's throw of the border with Detroit, the Grosse Pointe Police Department headquarters is a new, modern building with spiffy landscaping.

All of the cop cars and sleek new Ford sedans and Ford Explorers. One look at the police station and you understand that Grosse Pointe has a very solid and robust tax base.

I parked the car in one of the thirty-minute library parking spaces and hoped that it wouldn't take any longer than that. Inside, I turned right and went to the window where I introduced myself and said that I had an appointment to see the Chief. The door buzzed and I pushed my way through.

At the end of the hall, the last office on the left was the Chief's spot. I took a peek in and saw that the office was empty.

"Who let in this Peeping Tom?" I heard a voice say behind me.

As I turned, the Chief brushed past me and dropped into her chair behind the desk.

"This isn't good for my image, you know," she said. "Being seen with a known pervert."

The Chief's name was Ellen. Ellen Rockne. Yes, my sister. After my unfortunate break with the police in which I had to turn in my gun and badge, she had nonetheless persevered and made her way to the top. I was proud of her, but I would never tell her that. The Rockne clan would never be confused with a Hallmark feel-good made-for-tv special.

"Don't underestimate us," I said. "If not for perverts, you wouldn't have dated in high school."

She sighed. Ellen looked like me but without the typically pleasant expressions. When we grew up and the neighborhood bullies knew not to mess with Rockne, they weren't talking about me.

"What do you want, John? I've got an actual job, you know."

"Kierra Cotton," I said. "Who's in charge of her case?"

"The missing girl, right?" she said.

"That's the one."

"Now why would I give a nosy private investigator any details regarding an active investigation?" she said, flipping through a few files. She made her selection, opened it and did a quick scan.

Ellen raised an eyebrow and looked at me.

"Well, this particular private investigator is notoriously tight-lipped. Even under torture I never give up my sources," I said. "Plus, I'm only curious if the case has leads or if it's gone cold."

She snapped the file closed.

"Not cold. Room temperature."

I started to ask another question.

"You know what," she said. "You're not my favorite brother, so that's all you get. If you were my favorite, maybe I'd answer one more. But since you're not, I won't."

She got to her feet, the leather from her gun belt creaking.

I let myself out.

The part of Grosse Pointe that butts up against the border with Detroit is a collection of mostly rental properties known as the Cabbage Patch. The area is bordered on one side by Jefferson Avenue and the other by Alter Road. The entire area basically consists of twenty square blocks.

Lakepointe is in the middle of the Cabbage Patch and I parked my car in the midway between Jefferson and Mack.

I really couldn't think of any other way to try to find Antoine James. There was nothing online in any of the directories and no public records under his name or anyone with the last name of James that I could see owned property on Lakepointe.

So all I really had for AJ was his name, photo and the name of the street where he probably lived.

Having exhausted the more modern approaches to finding people it was time for an old-school approach. In other words, it was time for some good old-fashioned door-to-door detecting.

The first door I knocked on was the one directly to the right of my car. No better place to start than at the beginning, I figured.

In a folder at my side were some of the photos of AJ and Kierra I had printed off from the computer.

Using the brass knocker on the door, I rapped out a nice little rhythm. I waited, knocked again, but there was no answer.

One house at a time, I worked my way all the way to Mack, crossed the street and knocked on doors all the way back down the other side of Lakepointe, past where my car was parked. No one knew of AJ or Kierra, and no one could remember ever seeing anyone who looked like them.

It wasn't until I got to the last group of homes on Lakepointe that I got my first answer. A skinny old white guy with thick glasses and a goatee that looked like dried vomit told me that AJ's family lived two doors down from him.

"Best be on your toes," he said, just before slamming the door.

I was always on my toes. That explained my excellent posture.

Ignoring the man's pinpoint description, I went to the house next door and tried them first. There was no answer.

So with the photos in hand, I knocked on the door that supposedly belonged to AJ and his family.

It was a three-story home, split up into three apartments. It was made of brick, painted white, and there was a large flower pot on the porch with a few brown stems, the remains of a plant that most likely died about five years ago or so.

I rang the first bell and waited.

I rang the second bell.

"Yeah?" A man's voice said.

"Is AJ home?" I asked.

"Course not," he answered. Then, "Who's askin'?"

"A friend of Kierra's," I said. "She's missing."

"You a cop?"

"No."

A car drove by and I watched it turn onto Jefferson.

I heard footsteps on the stairs, and then a woman appeared behind the door. She had wild, straggly hair, sweat on her face and a huge gap between her teeth. In fact, it wasn't just a gap, she appeared to actually be missing several teeth. I smelled smoke and booze, not necessarily in that order.

She unlocked the door and opened it a crack.

"He ain't here," she said, her voice like rock scraping across concrete. Easy to see why I had misappropriated genders.

"Do you know where I might find him? Or do you have a cell phone number?"

She rotated her head from side to side. I actually *heard* her hair sway with the movement. "He always change phones anyway."

Her eyes squinted at me.

"You know about that place over on Wayborn?" she asked.

I acted as if I could almost place it.

"Yeah," I said. "I think I met him there once."

"He prob'ly there," she said.

"That's the place right over by...uh..." I looked up into the sky, desperately trying to remember something I never knew.

"Corner of Conner, behind that mall with the Foot

Locker and the Aldi," the woman said. "Where that girl got shot last week."

I snapped my fingers. "Oh yeah, that place. Of course."

Before I could ask another question, the door shut in my face and I heard the locks turn.

"Nice chatting, sir. I mean ma'am. I mean, sir-ma'am."

8

The border between Grosse Pointe and Detroit wasn't foreign to Clay. He had robbed a few rich people's homes in Grosse Pointe, where there were tons of cops, then scurried across Alter into Detroit, where you could call 911, claim a hundred terrorists were running around with rocket launchers, and the cops still wouldn't show up for an hour or two.

Wayborn was a side street off of Alter Road and it ran for nearly six blocks. Most of those blocks were completely deserted. The empty lots were overgrown with grass that was at least four feet high and weeds that were even taller. The grass was home to a booming population of pheasant, which could occasionally be seen crossing the street, probably heading for a liquor store.

Piles of garbage were strewn here and there, most in black trash bags, probably full of toxic shit the people from the suburbs didn't want to have to pay to get rid of. Much easier to just drive into Detroit after dark and give your unmentionables the old heave-ho.

Clay hated Detroit because it was full of scumbags. Most

of the deadbeats around the city were practically subhuman. Oh sure, they could be pretty clever occasionally, but hell he'd seen a YouTube video of a squirrel plucking out a rhythm on a giant harp. Who knew, maybe the assholes that were everywhere in *his* America would elect a squirrel President. The First Varmint. Wouldn't be much of a difference from the chump that was in there now, he thought.

Clay cruised in the Ram down the Detroit streets, driving right in the middle of the lane. If a car came toward him, he refused to move over and made them veer closer to the weedy lots. It wouldn't hurt their cars anyway, he reasoned. Most of the clunkers on the streets were full of rust, had broken windows, and looked like they'd been in a smash-up derby.

About the only thing he liked about Detroit, and this area in particular, was that you could sit for hours in a parked car and no one would think twice about it. Since there weren't any cops around, you could do whatever you wanted to. Places like this were the Wild West, and Clay thought of himself as a badass gunfighter.

So Clay had parked the Ram a block away from the house his new boss had noted on AJ's information. Ol' John Wayne had written down that this place was a possible drug house where his loser quarry sold most of his merchandise.

And someone was moving some serious dope out of that house, Clay could tell. The problem, he realized, was that all of these brothers with their pants hanging low and snapback baseball caps looked exactly alike. He looked again at the picture of AJ. Nothing really special. A narrow face. Big nostrils. He did have on a pair of glasses, though. Not many of the dudes going into the house had glasses.

Clay put the picture away.

He was getting bored. With the first of the cash, he had

swung into a liquor store and bought some smokes along with a pint of Early Times whiskey. What the hell kind of name was that for a whiskey? Early Times? That didn't sound good. He hated early times, especially in the morning. Who did they pay to think of these stupid-ass names? They should hire him. He'd take their big paycheck and sit in their fancy office and think of names for whiskey. Like...*Nice Ass Whiskey*. There, that was a great one. Couldn't you see the commercial? Two guys sitting around. Hey, I got some Nice Ass last night. The guy's buddy is jealous. The hero smiles knowingly.

Clay sighed. It would never happen. He'd never been able to hold down a steady job in his life. Plus, now he had to pee. And he was in the mood for something. What, he didn't know. But he usually felt it as a vibration. Most times, in the leg, and the leg would start twitching and he would be tapping his feet and pretty soon both legs were jumping around and his hands were tapping and then he'd realize he was grinding his teeth. When it got to that point, he'd find a bar, or a meth dealer, or a hooker. Or he'd pick a fight and beat the shit out of someone, or cut them up.

But he was on the job now.

Two more hours passed and both legs were now moving around and Clay was about to throw the Ram into gear and crack open the Early Times whiskey when a vintage Corvette pulled up in front of the house. A black guy climbed out. Wearing glasses.

No doubt.

It was AJ.

Clay put the Ram into gear and drove around the block so he could pull up right behind the Corvette.

He reached into the glovebox, pushed aside the pint of whiskey and pulled out the little .380 automatic, slid it into the front pocket of his jeans and touched the handle of the knife at the back of his waist. He also grabbed the lead-filled leather sap he had taken from an off-duty cop a couple years back. The idiot had actually tried to stop Clay from kicking around a stripper who'd foolishly held on to some of Clay's cash.

The cop lost a lot that night, including the sap. And the stripper lost more. As in, everything.

The sound of a voice from the house got a little louder and Clay slid from the truck, not shutting the driver's door all the way.

He was halfway up the cracked and weed-choked walkway when the door opened and AJ came out. He looked directly at him and Clay returned the stare. It was the normal thing to do. Clay noted AJ looked him up and down, saw the tattoos, knew he was probably being registered as a junkie.

They passed each other and as soon as AJ was past him, Clay quickly turned and swung with the sap, connecting with AJ's head just above his ear.

The sound was as solid and sick as Clay had ever heard. He loved that sound.

AJ started to go down but Clay caught him under the arm and dragged him to the Ram. He shoved him in the foot space on the passenger side and drove off, making a point to pull within inches of the fancy Corvette and snap off the car's side view mirror as he drove by.

The noise of it breaking off was his second favorite sound of the day.

9

As I drove toward the direction of the drug house the man-woman had told me about, I vaguely remembered the story of a shooting a week ago. It had happened just across the border from Grosse Pointe in Detroit.

Turned out a couple of Grosse Pointe high school students had bought some weed and pulled over on a dead end street to get high. Problem was, they were in Detroit. Last time I checked, they don't kid around in Detroit. So when a car pulled up behind them, they weren't ready. They weren't on guard. They were kids from Grosse Pointe who maybe thought it was exciting and daring to buy drugs in the bad city. But what happened was a guy with an assault rifle got out of the car and opened fire on the high schoolers. Maybe he'd followed them from the drug house. Maybe he was just a bad dude from the neighborhood and didn't like strangers in parked cars smoking weed. Or maybe he wanted to rob them.

One girl, sixteen years old, died immediately. One of the rounds had hit her directly in the head. Dead instantly. The kid behind the wheel somehow managed to pull the car out under the barrage of gunfire and get away. He drove directly to a nearby hospital's ER but it was too late for the girl. Two other kids were shot, but they survived.

There were no leads on who shot up the car.

So I made my way over, past the little shopping area with the Aldi store and a Foot Locker, into the desolated neighborhood behind it. There was a phrase local Detroiters use for people from the suburbs or out-of-towners who love to drive around and see what's happened to a once-great city. It's called "ruin porn." And as I drove around this area just across from Grosse Pointe, I could honestly understand the attraction. It's a fascinating, albeit sad and depressing, experience.

On the way to where I believed Wayborn Street was located, I passed an old school. Made of brick, it was a beautiful building. But when you looked a little more closely, all the windows were gone, the doors were padlocked even though all of the lower level windows were gone and anyone who heaved themselves up about three feet could get inside. The building was a stunning work of architecture, almost Frank Lloyd Wright prairie style. I had the urge to go inside and look around but knew there were most likely squatters and drug users inside who would be armed in some sense.

In other words, I wasn't *that* curious.

I found Wayborn one street over from the abandoned school.

Now, trap houses weren't exactly my specialty. In fact, being able to tell the difference between a house that sells drugs and one that hosts dog fights and one that has junkies hiding from cops and imaginary demons isn't all that easy.

The only way, really, is foot traffic.

And car traffic.

On cue, a big pickup truck with a scrawny white guy drove past me, giving me a death glare. He made a point of not moving over so I had to veer toward my side of the street to not get run over. I could see tattoos on the driver's arms and the expression on his face made him look like he wanted to kill me or rape me. Maybe both.

A white guy looking like that was most definitely looking for drugs, probably not illegal dumping.

The truck drove on and I caught the stench of heavy exhaust.

I continued on and saw a house that instantly met all of my criteria. Boarded up windows but a really stout door. A couple black guys were standing out front like they had just witnessed some kind of commotion. They were looking down the street where the truck had just passed me by.

They went back inside and I waited a few minutes then pulled up in front of the house.

There was no good way to do this.

I parked and went up to the door, knocked on it.

Even standing outside I could detect the stench of marijuana.

After a pause, someone spoke from inside.

"'Fuck you want?"

"Is AJ around?"

There was a little slot in the door and I shoved a twenty dollar bill through it. "I want to ask AJ about a girl he knows, Kierra. Goes by the name of Jade."

I heard footsteps behind me. I turned to see a white girl, way too thin, with a pretty face and a noticeable gap in her front teeth.

"You're going to get shot," she said. She had on skin-tight jeans, stiletto heels and a flimsy top.

On cue, a gun came out from the slot in the door. "Get the fuck out of here bro'."

I raised my hands and backed up. The girl took my spot at the door and I walked back to my car. I noticed a guy in the front window with what looked like an Uzi pointed at me.

I got back in my car and started it up. It seemed like a good idea to wait, to make sure the girl was okay even though on some level I knew that I was ill-equipped to protect her if anything went wrong.

But she made her purchase, turned around, and walked down the sidewalk, past my car with a bag in her hand.

As she walked past, she slid a business card through my window without breaking stride, and without anyone from the house being able to see the move.

I pulled away from the curb once I saw her get into her car and when I was out of view of the guys in the house with the guns, I glanced down at the paper.

It read:

Lace.

And a phone number.

10

*S*he couldn't move.

A gauzy white haze hung over her eyes. A deep, thrumming vibration washed over her and for a moment she wondered if she was near an airport or a train station but then she quickly realized the sound was coming from inside her. From deep within her chest.

It was a cry, a shriek of terror that came out as nothing more than a low, soft moan.

Her hands were tied.

Her feet were tied.

She didn't know where she was.

And she only had a vague idea of who she was.

Lost. That's what she was. Lost in every sense of the word with no hope of ever getting back.

Back to what?

Back to where?

Home? What she used to be? Who she used to be?

An onslaught of images and memories crashed into her mind, fought for space and clarity.

Nothing made sense anymore.
All she wanted to do was cry.
But she had forgotten how.

11

The next stop was my office. Crossing Alter and being back in Grosse Pointe was always an interesting feeling. Truth be told, I was never actually fearful in Detroit, but a heightened sense of alertness always made sense. However, it was a state of tension and afterward called for some relaxation strategies.

So once back in my office, I decided to lower my alert level via an ice cold beer. Inside my office fridge, I popped a top to a cold Dirty Blonde, brewed just down the street at Atwater Brewery and took a nice long drink. Nothing better than being alone in your office with a dirty blonde.

Thinking about the case made me want to organize some things on paper. So I brought out my notebook, flipped to a new page and jotted down everything that had happened so far, along with a to-do list. Number one on that list was getting ahold of Kierra's cell phone records. I had a few ideas on that one. Once I had my thoughts roughly organized, I pulled out the card with the girl's name and number from the trap house. Since she had been buying drugs at the time, I assumed, it occurred to me that it might be better to wait so I wouldn't catch her in the middle of a high. But then again I didn't really know her drug use schedule, so what the hell. No better time than the present.

I punched in the numbers and listened to it ring. Just when I thought it was going to voicemail a voice answered.

"'lo?"

"Hi," I said. "Is this Lace?"

There was a long pause and I thought I could hear music in the background and maybe soft breathing.

Should have listened to my instincts. If I'd ever heard someone whose breathing sounded really high, this was it.

"Hello?" I asked.

"Meet me at Bush Gardens," she said, in a voice just above a whisper. "I'll be there in a few hours." All the words sounded slurred together when she said them, but once I concentrated, I could make out what she was saying.

I was about to ask another question when the line disconnected.

For the kids at home, Bush Gardens is a strip club on 8 Mile Road in Detroit, not to be confused with the place in Florida where you can pet exotic species. Then again, having said that, I do realize there might be some similarities.

The Dirty Blonde hit empty, and I decided against another.

My computer was slow booting up but eventually I found my way to Google and did some more searching for Kierra, including using some special websites and databases known only to law enforcement. My sister Ellen had grudgingly allowed me access to the sites for my own personal endeavors and I put them to good use occasionally.

The good news was Kierra's name didn't come up in any of them. So she hadn't been arrested, incarcerated, or tagged in a morgue. The bad news was there was no record of her anywhere.

The clock said I was getting near dinnertime and I decided maybe the best idea would be to head home and grab a bite to eat before I made my way out to the strip club.

Telling Anna that my case was taking me out to 8 Mile wasn't a big deal. She knew that half the time I was going after criminals and let's face it, there was more than a fair share of criminals at strip clubs.

Still, sometimes it was a little weird to sit down to a delicious home-cooked meal and then head to a place full of naked women.

When I got home, everyone was already eating so I grabbed a plate, hugged everyone and sat down.

My two girls are naturally the apples of my eye. They couldn't be more different. Isabel, the oldest, was a highly verbal, first-born assertive leader at seven years old. Nina was a laid-back prankster at five years old. Life with the two of them and their feisty mother was a non-stop cavalcade of entertainment to me. They all cracked me up constantly. Of course, Anna sometimes got mad at me for taking great delight in whatever the girls did, good or bad. Maybe because I had seen death up close and personal that I tended to embrace the moment more than just about anyone I knew. It was very clear to me how quickly things could be taken away.

12

A fter dinner, I made sure all of the homework was either done or well on its way to being done, gave hugs and kisses all around and hopped back into the car.

Since there was no huge rush, I decided to take Lakeshore Drive on my way up to Vernier, which is what 8 Mile Road basically became once it passed over the freeway heading east toward Lake St. Clair. The lake was calm, with a beautiful silver sheen that set off the distant strip of horizon that was Canada. In this distance I could just make out the silhouette of a tanker heading north.

I turned left at the Grosse Pointe Yacht Club, then took Vernier into Detroit proper and made my way along 8 Mile Road. The street after which the famous movie (or infamous if you pay too much attention to the dialogue: 'I hear you're a real dope rapper...' was named doesn't have a lot to look at. A few strip malls, tiny bars, huge empty parking lots and strip clubs. Yes strip clubs. Quite a few of them, in fact. But you would never confuse them with say, strip clubs in Las Vegas. These were dark, dilapidated clubs that looked like someone had taken an abandoned dollar store and hired the clerks to dance.

Bush Gardens was a strange looking structure that looked like it been put together by someone who had salvaged new building supplies of all kinds and succeeded in using every one of them. There was a brick frame around the front façade, pale stucco panels, aluminum trim and even some bizarre copper cladding. There were some fake palm trees out front, the only nod to Florida's Busch Gardens that I could see.

I had to valet my car at the cost of eight dollars, even though there were a dozen empty parking spots within ten feet of the front door.

Inside, the thump of the giant subwoofers went right through me. I smelled a strange mixture of perfume slightly tinged with cigarette smoke.

"Need a booth?" a bouncer asked me. He had on a ridiculously tight polo shirt that revealed huge arms with bulging veins. His face was red and I thought if his body exploded, I wondered how much damage steroids and protein powder could do in an enclosed space.

"No thanks," I said.

There was a runway that went down the middle of the space, with tables right along the edge. On two slightly raised platforms on each side of the tables were booths. There were a couple of fat guys seated at different tables, and there was a black guy in one of the booths with about five strippers seated around him.

He either had money, drugs, or was just very, very lucky with the ladies.

At the bar, I ordered a light beer and turned to the stage. A woman way too old to be a stripper was on her knees doing something with her ass that looked more like an exercise to relieve hip pain than anything sexual.

I didn't see any other dancers in the stage area so I glanced over at the booth where all the action seemed to be taking place. It was hard to tell in the dim light, but I was pretty sure that Lace was sitting two girls away from the black guy.

There were quite a few things in the world I certainly didn't know about. Britney Spears' bra size. Donald Trump's toupee manufacturer. Or how to field dress a wildebeest, for instance.

I did know, however, that in strip clubs money talked and bullshit walked.

So I flagged down a girl carting drinks around, slipped her two twenties, and told her to keep one and give the other to Lace and I raised my chin toward the booth.

When my messenger completed her task, everyone in the booth turned to look at me and then turned back and several of them started laughing.

The black guy was the only one who didn't even smile.

Lace got up and walked toward me. She looked stoned out of her mind and I wondered what the odds were that she would even remember me. She had on a tiny red dress that barely covered her lower parts and showed most of her upper parts. In addition to the dress she wore a pair of ridiculous shoes that were made of clear plastic and added about six inches to her height. But her skin was practically translucent and she was shivering. Zero percent body fat will do that to you.

She came up, slipped both arms around me and whispered in my ear.

"Let's go in the back."

Lace took me by the hand and we walked past the booth,

past the old stripper on stage to the back rooms that were enclosed by red curtains. Another bouncer came out.

"It's ten for a booth," he said. I fished out a ten, handed it to him, and Lace maneuvered her way to a corner booth, wobbling slightly, at the back of the enclosed space.

I sat down on the little leather bench and Lace pulled the curtain closed behind her. She started taking off her dress.

"Whoa!" I said. "No need to disrobe."

"It's still twenty-five," she said and then promptly sat on my lap.

"Do I know you?" she asked.

"Yeah, you gave me your card. I think you heard me asking about Kierra."

Her eyes were at half-mast but at the sound of Kierra's name they widened enough to look almost normal.

"Why were you asking about Kierra?" she said.

"I'm trying to find her. Do you know anything about her?"

She leaned back and looked at me.

"Dances are thirty bucks," she said.

I almost said something about her earlier quoted price being twenty-five, but decided against it. She weighed next to nothing and the gap in her teeth looked bigger.

I gave her forty.

"She used to dance here," she said, jamming the bills somewhere down below. "Went by the name of Jade. We were friends and I'm trying to find her, too. I wouldn't have said anything to you but you look like a nice guy," she said.

I had pretty much guessed that Lace was going to tell me Kierra had worked here, but was still surprised at how thoroughly Kierra had hidden her secret job from her parents and her social media accounts. I hadn't seen a single picture or reference to the club.

"When was the last time you saw her?"

Lace shrugged her paper-thin shoulders. "A week or two ago? I don't know. I have trouble keeping track of time."

"Did Kierra use drugs, too?" I said.

It would have been laughable if she had denied it and I saw her almost start to, then realize there was no point. "Yeah, she did, too. I felt kind of responsible because I was supposed to be a little bit of a mentor to her when she started dancing."

She laughed.

"Me? Taking care of someone else?" she laughed again and for a brief moment I saw a sweet, pretty girl behind the obvious signs of drug abuse.

"Did she say anything to you the last time you saw her? Say where she was going? Who she was going with?" I pressed.

"No," Lace said. "She mentioned her grandfather a couple of times, though. They must have been close."

Grandfather? That was strange. Why hadn't Marvin said anything to me about the fact that his daughter was so close to her grandfather? Strange detail to leave out.

"That guy in the booth?" I asked. "Is he your dealer?"

She giggled and the music stopped briefly.

"You have to pay me again if you want to keep talking."

Two more twenties went into her hand and then disappeared.

She looked at me, and started grinding a little bit to the music. Probably already anticipating the high she was going to get with the money I'd given her.

"You don't have to do that," I said. "That guy out there, is he your dealer?" I repeated.

"No. You make it sound so formal," she laughed again. "I buy when I can and from who I can. No real strategy."

"What about Kierra? Did she buy drugs from that guy?"

"I don't think so. Jade bought from a guy called....I don't remember. Initials. KJ, maybe?"

"Or AJ?"

She shrugged again.

"I liked Jade," she said. "She was my friend. I miss her."

I pulled one of my business cards out and gave it to her. "I know someone who could help you," I said. "If you want to get out of this life."

Lace's eyes flashed. "If you want to give me a tip, make it cash. Otherwise fuck off."

Another twenty went into her hand and I got to my feet.

"Call me if you think of anything else."

13

About halfway to the warehouse the black punk started to wake up so Clay waited until he was free of traffic, pulled out the sap, and pounded the asshole's head until his eyes rolled back into his head and he slumped back into the foot space.

"Nighty night," Clay said.

If you were a person who had an occasional need for an abandoned property, especially a warehouse, there was no better city in the world than Detroit. For starters, the auto industry collapsed years ago and all the jobs went to Mexico or China. Clay knew this because his own kind had all lost their jobs and either fled up to northern Michigan to crank out meth, or back home to Kentucky and Alabama to resume their redneck ways.

All those abandoned car factories were everywhere in Detroit, especially downriver, where Clay had cut his teeth becoming a career criminal. What most people didn't realize, though, was that all of the businesses that had supported the auto industry collapsed, too.

Companies that built the little door hinges, or sheet

metal or any of the little millions of pieces that went into manufacturing a car had all gone belly up, too. And all of those places had their own warehouses and storage sheds that were now vacant, and guarded only by a fence with maybe a single strand of barbed wire. Hell, the bank owned all of that shit and they didn't have time for actual security.

Clay's base of operations was an abandoned property a couple miles from the airport in Romulus. He had discovered it when he was trying to get rid of a body and the sign, Universal Tool & Die had appealed to his sense of humor.

He'd made his own little entrance through a disguised section of chain-link fence that was completely obstructed. The time and energy was well spent because he'd found an in-ground cistern full of waste chemicals that now had four bodies in various stages of decomposition.

Soon to be five, Clay thought.

He got out of the Ram, unlocked his makeshift garage door, and pulled the truck through. He went back, shut the chain-link door, and rolled a mini-dumpster in front of the opening, locking the wheels in place.

There were at least five abandoned structures on the property, but the best one was in the back. Clay drove the Ram around the back of the building and parked between the back wall and a stack of pallets he'd piled in order to block any views if someone happened to traipse through the field of weeds and scrub brush that went on for nearly a quarter mile to a farmer's tree line.

The back door to the building had been locked, naturally, but Clay had broken in and then jerry-rigged his own lock, which he now unfastened with a key from his keychain. He opened the door, stepped inside, took a quick look to make sure no homeless people had found a way in – that would be their very, very bad luck – then went back to the Ram and dragged the black kid inside. He closed the door behind him, and locked it from the inside.

Clay grabbed the kid by an ankle and dragged him to the center of the room where he had some heavy chain draped over a steel ceiling truss, a chair, and a pair of handcuffs. He fastened the handcuffs around the kid, then ran the chain through them in a loop, which he secured with a padlock. Clay kicked the chair away so it would be well out of reach of his captive, who was now slumped on his side with his arms above him.

A bucket held some dirty water and Clay splashed it into the kid's face. His eyes opened, and Clay clobbered him with the empty metal pail.

The kid's eyes opened all the way.

"Look down at your feet," Clay said.

The black asshole looked down. The water from the bucket was swirling down a drain that was built into the floor.

Around the drain were streaks of black.

"That's dried blood," Clay said. He pulled the pint of Early Times from his back pocket and took a long drink.

And then he laughed.

14

On the way home from Bush Gardens I pulled out my cell phone and dialed Marvin Cotton. I told him I had interviewed an acquaintance of Kierra's, leaving out the fact that she was a co-worker at a strip club on 8 Mile, and told him that said person had indicated Kierra had been extremely close with her grandfather.

"Sorry, but that's bullshit," Marvin Cotton said. "My old man saw Kierra once in awhile but not much. He isn't exactly the warm-and-feely kind of guy."

It was the first confirmation of what I'd expected would probably be a pattern; that Lace's information was going to be mostly inaccurate. A drugged-out stripper didn't always make the best source. I was trying not to be judgmental, but drugs and the truth tended not to last long as roommates.

"I mean, the old man lives in Lansing," Marvin continued. The way he said it made it sound like Lansing was halfway to Pluto.

"There's no way she's been making side trips to Lansing without any of us knowing about it."

My silence told him I didn't agree.

"I mean, you can go talk to him if you want," Marvin said. "He doesn't have a phone or a cell phone, so that's really the only way. Face-to-face. But I guarantee it'll be a waste of gas."

"That's okay, mileage is tax-deductible," I said. Ever since I'd spent the money on a new accountant, I was determined to get my money's worth.

Marvin gave me the address for his father in Lansing, I thanked him, and we disconnected.

I went home and took a long, hot shower. From just the few minutes Lace had been sitting on my lap, I reeked of perfume.

It was a listless night's sleep, tossing and turning so much that at one point Anna gave me an elbow in the ribs.

The next morning, I was up but not rested. The sun was already up by the time I got to my office and the Kroger just a few doors down was busy with people going in and out of the store. A tired-looking high school kid was rounding up stray shopping carts with an understandable lack of enthusiasm.

My reserved parking space was one of only three behind my building. The other two belonged to a couple of stock-brokers from the tiny Merrill Lynch office next door. One drove a Porsche Panamera – that was the sedan. Which made no sense to me. Who wants to drive a Porsche that looks like a boring family car? The other car next to mine was a white Range Rover.

To be honest, the best-looking car, though, was my seven-year-old Honda minivan. It was sleek, a total chick magnet, and it was paid for. I'm joking about the first two, but the last one is the reason I love it. Plus, a minivan is awesome for surveillance because no one notices it and if it's an especially long stakeout, you can fold all the seats down and stretch out.

So I fired her up and headed out toward Lansing. An easy drive by just hopping on I-96 and heading west.

Lansing was the state capitol and a small city I really liked. It was home to Michigan State University and the countryside surrounding was mostly agricultural with the occasional horse ranch thrown in.

The address Marvin had given me went into my phone's navigation app, and I followed it without deviation until a little more than an hour later I pulled up in front of a small bungalow on a quiet street a few blocks over from the main square in Lansing.

I parked in front of the house, locked it, and walked up to the front door.

After I rang the bell, it took a few minutes before the door opened. Marvin Cotton, with the addition of about forty years, looked back at me.

"Mr. Cotton? My name is John Rockne and your son hired me to look into the disappearance of his daughter," I said in my friendliest voice. The kind of voice that made people *want* to invite me in, as opposed to *having* to invite me in. "Would it be all right if I asked you a few questions?"

He looked at me with eyes that were rimmed with red from age, as opposed to smoking controlled substances. Finally, he seemed to come to a judgment of sorts and opened the door for me.

"Come on in," he said. "Want some coffee?"

"No thanks."

The house smelled like cigar smoke and old men. Which made sense because there were three old men sitting around a card table and one of them had a cigar going.

They all looked at me.

"Good morning, gentlemen," I said.

One or two of them may have grumbled a hello but they all turned back to the card game.

"George you gonna finish the hand or what?" one of them barked at Marvin Cotton's Dad. I knew this not because I knew Grandpa Cotton's first name, but because the other old man was glaring right at him.

"Hell no," George said. "I've taken enough of your damn money. You'll be eating that beagle of yours back home if I keep whuppin' your ass."

George Cotton waved me back toward what appeared to be the kitchen.

"Come in here," he said. "What'd you say your name was?"

"John."

I followed him through a small kitchen to a back door that led out to a tiny patio with two chairs.

George Cotton sat in one, slowly and painfully, and pointed to the other.

"Figured you wouldn't want to breathe all that smoke," he said. "You look like a dandy."

That made me laugh. That would have made Anna laugh even harder. I bought my clothes at JCPenney. *A frickin' dandy?*

Ha.

"I appreciate that."

The backyard was the size of a postage stamp but neat, with a charcoal smoker off to one side and a metal pail just beyond. For cigar butts, I figured.

"So did you know Kierra was missing?" I said.

"No. I only talk to Marvin once in awhile. He's still mad at me for being too tough on him." The old man's face sort of crinkled when he said it and I couldn't tell if the expression was from disgust or the fact that he found some humor in the words.

"When was the last time you saw Kierra?" I asked.

"How long has she been missing?"

Nothing bugs a private investigator more than someone who answers questions with a question. But I love old people, so I gave him a break.

"A few weeks."

He nodded. "She's about that age, I suppose."

"What age would that be?"

"Where they can't take being at home anymore. Like caged animals. Her Dad was like that. Oh, yes sir," he said. "He stormed on out of the house, told me to kiss his black ass. Then about six months later he was begging to come home."

The old man laughed. He was a tough old guy, I could tell.

"So when was the last time you saw Kierra?" I asked again.

A bird flew overhead and landed in a tree in the neighbor's yard. George Cotton's eyes followed its flight and squinted at it, as if he was daring it to land in his yard.

"Three, four years ago, I guess," he finally said. "Marvin had a big barbecue to celebrate their new house. He overcooked the ribs. Too tough. The meat should always fall off the bone."

I rolled my eyes. Marvin had been right. This was a waste of time.

"Did you keep in touch with her other ways? Phone? Email?"

He actually let out what could only be described as a guffaw. "Son, you drove out here probably because my son told you I don't have a phone. If I don't have a phone, then you know I don't have a computer or whatever they use for those electric mail things, am I right?"

"You're right," I admitted. For a brief moment, I thought he might tell me what a crummy private investigator I was. Right up there with Marvin's ability to grill meat.

"George! Get your sorry ass back in here," one of the guys inside the house called out. "Quit hiding from me."

"Chester just leave your money on the table, you know I'm going to take it from you, anyway. Just like I done with your woman."

One of the old guys let out a howl and George winked at me.

I stood up and shook his hand.

"Thank you for chatting with me, Mr. Cotton," I said, giving him my card. "Call me if you do hear from Kierra. Maybe you can borrow a phone from one of your buddies."

He waved the idea away like it was a troublesome fly. "She'll probably come home in a few weeks," he said. "They always do."

15

On the way out of Lansing, I realized I hadn't eaten breakfast so I stopped at a Starbucks and grabbed a coffee and a blueberry scone. Blueberry because I knew I could count the scone as one serving of fruit. Very healthy, in other words.

Back on the freeway headed for Detroit, I called up my reporter friend Nate but it was sent straight to voicemail and decided not to leave a message. I had known Nate my whole life. He was a journalist, having worked as a reporter for the Grosse Pointe newspaper for most of his career. He had since moved onto the Detroit Free Press.

The great thing about Nate was that he had an incredible memory for names and faces which was not only great for his career, and probably part of the reason he went into reporting, but it was also great for me. Selfish, I know. But Nate Becker was a great help to me and a resource I utilized frequently.

By not leaving a message Nate would know that I was calling because I wanted some help from him, but I was happy to be able to convey the request without having to get roped into buying him lunch just to pose the question. Nate was a big guy and he loved his food so my payments to him for his help were meals. Big meals. Really, really big meals.

As I passed fields of corn and vast swatches of green I kept my eye out for deer. Not so much in case they jumped a fence and volunteered to become a hood ornament, but because I loved spotting them. "Deer!" I would shout out to the empty car. I'm very easily entertained.

No sign of anything interesting on the drive back, which paired nicely with the fact that I hadn't found anything of interest at George Cotton's place. Well, most of the time in my business it was wrong to think of information as a "lead" because it rarely led you anywhere worthwhile.

Still, it was kind of a weird thing for Lace to have made up. Why would she have told me that Kierra had a close relationship with her grandfather if it hadn't been true? I knew Lace wouldn't be a reliable source, but it seemed like such an odd thing for her to lie about. I knew she was on drugs, probably drank a lot, and was out of it half the time. But typically that resulted in misinformation more in the sense of just being wrong, or mistaken. Not fabricating stories for no reason. Unless she had a reason for sending me off in a false direction? Or had she just been pissed off I hadn't wanted a "dance."

Still, I couldn't stop noodling it around. Had she meant something else, or *someone* else? Had Kierra known a different "George" and Lace assumed it was her friend's grandfather? Would Kierra have told Lace her grandfather's first name? Highly unlikely. And certainly more unlikely that Lace would have remembered it.

Suddenly, I found myself thinking back to Kierra's social media accounts. A nudge, or a wiggle or whatever you want to call it. A brain passing-of-gas, perhaps.

But had I seen something there?

Without any real reason why, I made it back to my office in record time, parked the van next to the Porsche and hurried up to my desk. I roused the computer from sleep, launched the web browser and promptly logged into Kierra's Instagram account.

I grabbed a Diet Coke from the fridge and sipped as I scanned the pictures, not even sure what I was looking for. I had already looked at all of the pictures several times. Mostly shots of Kierra with people at clubs, or friends sticking their tongues out at the camera. Why do young people do that? What is it about a camera that makes them want to hang their tongues out of their mouths like camels?

If Anna was with me, she'd tell me I was acting like an old man again. Oh, well.

Right then, a picture on her Instagram made me stop. It was a photo of Kierra with a guy who had on a black baseball cap, a chain around his neck with a D emblem representing Detroit, and making a peace sign toward the camera.

I glanced at the caption Kierra had added to the photo. And smiled. *Why did I ever doubt myself?*

The caption read simply: "Clubbin' out with my man, Grandmaster D!"

16

The driveway was home to my wife's car and another vehicle I didn't recognize. I ended up parking on the street and letting myself in the side door.

A woman sat at our kitchen table with Anna, each clutching oversized coffee cups. I knew my wife wouldn't be drinking coffee in the afternoon and sure enough, the smell of green tea tinged with honey reached my finely honed senses.

"John, this is Arnella Cotton," Anna said. She smiled at me, but I could tell the smile wasn't the usual look of sheer joy she usually wore when she saw me. Kidding, of course.

"Hi Arnella," I said, shaking hands with her. Her hand was warm and sweaty either from the tea or nerves.

"Hello, Mr. Rockne," she said.

"Please. Call me John."

"Ok, call me Arnella."

Arnella Cotton was a short, plump woman with a breathtakingly beautiful face. I knew where Kierra had gotten her good looks, that was for sure.

"A tea party? And I wasn't invited?" I said to my wife. I gave Anna a peck on the cheek.

"There's plenty of water left," my wife said, nodding at the teapot still on the stove. I went over to the coffeemaker, saw there was a little left in the bottom and poured myself a cup, then popped it into the microwave.

"Thanks, but I need some real caffeine," I said. "How are you holding up, Arnella?"

The woman glanced up at me and shrugged her shoulders. "About as well as I could be expected to, I guess." She had a voice that was deeper than expected and a bit of an edge to her tone. "The hardest thing for a mother is not knowing where your child is and what has happened, or is happening, to her."

Anna reached over and put her hand on Arnella's. "John will find her, Mrs. Cotton, I know he will." She glanced over at me and gave me that look that said, you better not make a liar out of me.

Luckily, the microwave dinged and I turned around, took out the cup, had a test sip and pulled up a chair next to the ladies.

"Is that why you're here?" I asked.

"Yes and no," Arnella said. "Yes, I am worried, but no, I don't want you to look for her anymore."

This was a shock to me.

"You don't want me to?" I asked.

"Look, my husband is a good man," Arnella said. "But he's got a temper. Especially when it comes to his daughter. Marvin was raised in a very strict family and he wanted to do the same with his."

I thought back to George Cotton and I understood what she was getting at.

"Marvin and Kierra clashed. A lot. And…" she paused as

she searched for the right word. "Severely," she finished. "They clashed severely."

"You mean physically?" I asked.

Arnella shook her head. "No, no. Never. The fights just got ugly. Real ugly."

When she took a drink of her tea I asked, "So what you're saying is that you think nothing bad happened to her. You think Kierra just ran away because of the fights with Marvin. That she needed some space. That she's not really missing."

I was guessing, of course, but that could only be the logical path Arnella was taking.

"I'm ninety-nine percent sure that's what happened," she confirmed.

"But don't you want John to make sure that extra one percent isn't something to worry about?" my wife added. "And I'm not asking because he needs work, it's just that as a mother and I can only imagine how difficult this must be for you."

Anna is an Italian beauty, not sure if I mentioned that before. But in the light of the kitchen, with those big brown eyes so full of compassion, she looked spectacularly beautiful. Man, I was lucky.

"Actually, I could use the work," I joked.

Wrong thing to say. Anna's eyes went from caring to pit viper-ish in a nanosecond.

"Just kidding," I added.

"I came here to release you from the case," Arnella said. "I think Kierra will be home soon and I don't want Marvin stressing out about it anymore."

"Well, I do appreciate you coming here," I said. "But Marvin is my client and only Marvin can terminate my services."

Now it was Arnella's face that changed.

"You're telling me my husband is the only one–"

"Yes, unfortunately," I persisted. "But if you just want to have him call me..."

She stood up abruptly and looked at me.

"He and I don't agree with this so he won't call you. And if I don't have any say in the matter I might as well go." She looked at Anna. "I appreciate the tea and the conversation."

"My pleasure," Anna said.

We both watched her walk out the door.

My wife turned to me.

"Let's talk about your client service skills, John."

I t could be that with the kids off at school, Anna and I may have fooled around a bit after Arnella Cotton left.

Or, more accurately, it could be that my better half just made me take out the trash and bring the laundry baskets up from the basement. I'll let your imagination run with those two scenarios.

A quick check of Grandmaster D told me that he was a rap musician (with slight funk overtones according to one article) and owner of Destroy Records in downtown Detroit.

I decided the best bet would be to just drive down there and check this guy out. Especially after I found a phone number and the call just rang without even going to a voicemail.

One of the perks of living in Grosse Pointe is being able to zip down to Detroit without having to get on the freeway. Jefferson Avenue is one of my favorite streets in Detroit as it winds along Lake St. Clair and then the Detroit River, passing by Belle Isle and some fascinating parts of the city.

Without much traffic to deal with I made it downtown in ten minutes or so, and found a parking spot near the building that supposedly housed Destroy Records. One great thing about Detroit, especially compared to other cities, is the plethora of parking options. The city is actually on the way up, in my opinion, and parking isn't as abundant as it once was. But compared to places like Chicago or Boston? Not even close.

The building matching the address on my phone was vintage Detroit. Probably built in the '20s or '30s, and had most likely been abandoned at some point. The structure was about six stories high and the upper floors bore hall-marks of classic Art Deco design.

The street level had obviously seen several incarnations but it looked like someone had tried to strip away some of the façade and find the original face of the building, without much success.

A giant door made of brushed metal represented the entrance, and its surface featured a raised D in the style of the Detroit Tigers logo.

There was an intercom on the right with a white button so I pushed it.

Nothing happened.

I pushed it again.

Nothing happened.

I grabbed the big metal door's handle and pulled.

It opened.

It made me a little nervous to just walk into a building in Detroit without being invited. I didn't have my gun. Just my cell phone and a pack of Wintergreen gum.

At least I would die with fresh breath.

"Hello?" I called out as I stepped inside.

It was dark, and got even darker as the door swung shut behind me. The floor was wood, stained black, and the lobby, if you wanted to call it that, was completely empty.

There were two hallways, one on each side of the open space with no indication as to what those would lead to.

I heard footsteps and from the hallway on the left a Rottweiler appeared with a huge silver chain around its neck.

A soft but incredibly deep growl emanated from its chest. That growl corresponded with a stab of fear in my belly. Ordinarily I love dogs, but when one that big growls, well, it scares the crap out of me.

From behind the beast of Satan, a woman appeared. She had on a tight black dress that failed entirely to contain her curves. A dozen rolls of duct tape would probably fail at that job, too.

"Can I help you?" she said. Her voice was filled with honey. "Stop it, Boss," she said to the dog.

Boss bowed his enormous head and retreated silently into the hallway, giving me one more glance over his shoulder. If he could talk, he was saying, "I've got my eye on you, white boy."

"I was hoping to meet with Grandmaster D," I said, the name sounding strangely formal. "I have some questions for him about a case I'm investigating."

"You're not a cop," she pointed out. "Sure as hell don't look like one."

"Nope, private investigator."

An expression briefly flitted across her face that told me she considered my job title to be on par with that of a porta-potty attendant.

She gave me a withering expression, then followed the path the dog had taken into the hallway and a few minutes later a man appeared. He was tall, at least a couple inches over six feet, and lean. But the lean part of him was all muscle.

"Can I help you?" he said. He approached and stopped right in front of me. He made no move to shake my hand. I was about to offer mine but thought better of it. Up close, his face was angular and shaped by dark edges.

"Yes, I'm John Rockne, a private investigator. I'd like to ask Grandmaster some questions about a case I'm working on."

"And what is the nature of the case?" When he spoke, I caught a glimpse of perfect white teeth. He folded his arms across his chest and I could see the ropy muscles in his forearms.

Suddenly, the dog seemed like a friendlier acquaintance.

"It's about a missing girl. Her name is Kierra Cotton but some people call her Jade."

His flat black eyes didn't change one bit. Either he didn't know the name, or a blank death stare was his natural mode of expression.

"Grandmaster D isn't here but I'm happy to take a message for you."

It was my turn to smile. He could have told me Grandmaster wasn't here *before* he asked me about the case. So why did he want to know?

"Sure, I can leave a message," I said. "And what is your name?"

He smiled, but it wasn't the kind of smile that warmed your cockles, whatever cockles are.

"Nix," he said.

I handed him one of my business cards.

"I'd like to talk with him if he ever has an opening in his schedule."

"He's an extremely busy man," Nix said.

If there was a wastebasket in the place, I had a feeling my business card was about to find it very soon.

"It would be great if he could find some time," I said, then decided to push it. "He and Kierra seemed very close, at least according to her Instagram account."

Nix looked like he was going to ask me something and then stopped. My guess is that he knew who I was talking about, which made me very interested.

"He takes lots of picture with lots of people," Nix said.

"I have a feeling he would remember her," I countered.

The dog appeared behind Nix and started growling.

Or it might have been Nix himself, which wouldn't have surprised me.

"I'll see he gets the message," Nix said.

He used the kind of tone of voice that told me he hoped I was getting his message, too. Which I was.

Loud and clear.

18

Knives were an important part of Clay's family history. The blade was nearly as important as a hatred for law, a disdain for authority and willingness to take what rightfully wasn't yours.

The Arkansas Toothpick, the Bowie, the switchblade. Throwing knives, skinning knives, survival knives. They had all at one point or another passed through Clay's hands.

Now, with his captive fully awake and aware of the situation he was in, Clay went to the small cooler near the back door, opened it, and pulled out a can of Pabst. The bottle of Early Times was gone, and besides, something cold was better for this kind of work.

Cutting always made him thirsty.

He popped the tab and walked over to where AJ slumped.

Clay took a drink of his beer.

"You might not think it, but you do have some options," he said.

AJ slowly raised his head and looked at Clay.

"You can tell me what I want to know now and I'll let you go," Clay said. "Or you can tell me what I want to know later, after I've used this on you."

He held up the knife in front of AJ's face.

"This is called a gut-hook skinning knife," Clay said. "See how the blade has a slight curve? That's for the skinning."

AJ looked down at the floor drain.

"See that little notch there at the end?" Clay asked. He smiled and took a drink from his Pabst.

"That's the gut hook. It's fucking razor-sharp, man."

Clay flicked his wrist, and cut a two-inch long gash in AJ's forearm.

"Fuck!" AJ yelled out.

"See what I mean?" Clay laughed. "Look at how that bitch cut right through and I didn't even apply any pressure. Shit! This is a damn good knife, boy."

"I'll tell you whatever the fuck you want to know," AJ said. "But I have to tell you I don't know who the hell you are or why you have me here. I don't know anything about anyone. I'm just a guy who sells some weed once in awhile and who likes to party. That's it, nothing more."

Clay set the can of Pabst on the floor and stepped closer to AJ.

"I think you're a lying piece of shit," Clay said. "And I don't believe a word you just said. But it doesn't matter. All I want to know is where the girl is. Jade. Where is she?"

"Oh, no," AJ said. He started weeping.

"What's wrong, crybaby?"

AJ swung his head from side to side. "I don't know where she is," he said, in between sobs. "She disappeared. I've been looking for her, too."

"I'm so happy you chose option two," Clay said.

Moments later, AJ's screams filled the room as his blood poured down the floor drain.

19

Nate called me back and I reluctantly agreed to meet him for dinner. I had a fancy new corporate card, though, so it would be easier to keep track of my receipts for the tax man. Since most of what we discussed would be work-related, all of my meals with Nate would be legitimate business expenses. It was the only way I could survive these outings without an ulcer or two.

A new burger place had opened on Kercheval and luckily Nate had agreed to it. Which was great for me because even though my friend's appetite was extreme, you could only do so much damage at a burger joint. Financially speaking, of course. Medically speaking, well, that was a whole different story.

I found Nate sitting in the back booth and slid in across from him.

"Check this out," he said, pointing at the menu. "The Blue Note – it's new." I took a glance, saw it was a double decker burger with blue cheese.

"Cool," I said. "Better name than say, the Blueger, which sounds kind of gross."

Nate was a heavyset guy with a thick beard and even thicker glasses. He was married with one daughter, a girl who had been born without a pulmonary artery, which had been a fairly major surprise at the time. Since then, and several operations later, she was doing fine. The medical bills were still there, even though Nate had been chipping away at them for years now.

The waiter came by and took our drink orders. Coke for Nate, unsweetened ice tea for me.

"So what's new?" I asked him.

"Same old stuff, John," my friend said wearily. "University of Michigan football team is front-page news, murders and widespread government corruption barely get a mention."

"If the football team was corrupt, then you've got a story," I offered.

"All big-time college sports are corrupt," he pointed out. "Most of the guys graduate barely being able to read and write."

There was no point arguing with him, he was right, for the most part.

"What's new with you?" he asked.

"I wrapped up a divorce case. This guy who had a couple of patents for injection molding thought his wife was cheating on him and she was. I documented her dalliances and it ended up being a pretty fair divorce all around."

"He keep his patents?"

"Yep. She found some other guy's injections more interesting," I guess.

Nate groaned.

"I know, too easy," I admitted. "Anyway, I'm working right now on a missing persons case, a young woman. Kierra Cotton."

Nate shook his head to indicate he didn't recognize the name. Grosse Pointe was a very small community but you couldn't possibly know *everyone.*

"I'm going to try the Blue Note and the Western," he said.

I nodded in response. Nate was overweight and I had made the mistake once of trying to help. Bad idea. Apparently he got enough of that at home and extra scrutinizing from his oldest friend wasn't welcome.

So I kept my mouth shut regarding the issue.

Which, for me, was an accomplishment.

The waiter arrived on cue and Nate told him what he wanted and I added my regular – a cheeseburger with fried onions and sweet potato fries. That was my new thing. Sweet potato fries. Another thing I had convinced myself was way healthier than the regular deal.

"Ever heard of a local rapper named Grandmaster D?" I asked.

"Sure," Nate answered. "He's a fairly well-respected musician and producer. I think he's known more for his producing. Probably making more money that way, too."

"I went to talk to him today but his security guy cut me off at the pass. Quite thoroughly I might add. He said his name was Nix. Ever heard of him?"

"Doesn't ring a bell. But I don't think this is the kind of guy you just show up and talk to," Nate said. "I'm sure he's got plenty of people around him. Does he have something to do with the missing girl?"

"I think so. She apparently talked a lot about him with a stripper friend and there are a lot of pictures of him on her Instagram."

"Stripper?" He raised an eyebrow. "How old is this missing girl?"

"Just out of high school."

He shook his head. "Everything is getting worse and the victims are getting younger and younger." He looked at me. "Was she hooking, too?"

"No way," I said, thinking back to my conversation with Lace. She hadn't said anything about prostitution.

"Are you sure about that, John?" he asked me.

"Why?"

He shrugged his shoulders. "What club was she stripping at?"

"Bush Gardens."

Nate's mouth turned up at the corner. "She was hooking, then."

The waiter came and put down our food. I realized I was going to be sharing Nate's attention with the two massive burgers now sitting in front of him.

"How can you be so sure?" I asked.

"Because Bush Gardens is a fucking brothel, John. Everyone knows that," my friend said as he tore into his first burger. After a few chews to get the first piece down, he continued. "Practically every club on 8 Mile is. The dancing is just a pretense. The real business goes on in back in those booths. Blow jobs, straight fucking, anything you want. And most girls are there to lure customers in, and then they start meeting them outside the club, at hotels, even though the club's owner probably doesn't like that, but it's a cost of doing business."

I'd heard those rumors, but I'd always been a little skeptical. I could see Lace doing some things in that room we'd been in if the price was right, but Kierra? Even when she was Jade? I had my doubts.

And then I wondered if the reason Lace had gotten so pissed off at me at the end of our conversation was because I hadn't ordered any "extras." Suddenly, I felt embarrassed and slightly offended.

"She might have been with a service, too," Nate added, after he'd already devoured the Blue Note.

I wondered if it was Nate's training as a reporter that always made him think the worst.

"So in addition to stripping, possibly turning tricks in some slimy booth at a strip club, meeting customers for sex, she might have been working at an escort service?" I asked. "Is that what you're saying?"

Nate nodded instead of answering. His jaws were busy destroying the Western burger.

I thought of Marvin Cotton and Arnella. And suddenly, I lost whatever appetite I'd had.

20

W e chatted for awhile longer and Nate agreed to see if he could find out anything more about Grandmaster D, then we said our goodbyes. I sent Anna a quick text to let her know I'd had dinner with Nate and was going to the office for a couple of hours.

Since the burger place was only a few blocks from my office, I decided to walk it. The main street of Grosse Pointe typically saw a lot of turnover in terms of stores and restaurants. I'd heard that it was mostly because the real estate was owned by one person who charged abnormally high rents. Luckily, my building was owned by a former client who rented my space to me for very little.

I went inside, climbed the stairs and unlocked my office. I shut all the blinds, turned on my computer and found a good blues album in iTunes.

Once the computer was ready, I began searching escort services in Detroit.

The results were overwhelming.

Most of the sites listed seemed fake, as if they were just aggregators that pulled together other fake ads.

The most prominent site was backpage.com which seemed to be the do-it-yourself escort service. However, after taking a look at the photos and comparing them to some of the "professional" sites, it looked like some of those same companies were advertising on backpage as if they were amateurs.

It was a safe assumption that the whole escort industry was a swamp full of bullshitters. Wasn't that why people wanted to legalize prostitution? So it could be regulated and taxed?

The page of photos on my screen made me dizzy. It was a swarm of asses, really. Women mostly bent over. A lot of shots in the bathroom using the mirror. Was that a big turn-on for men? An attractive woman in bra and panties standing next to a clearly visible toilet? Were toilets aphrodisiacs these days?

Occasionally, someone would mix up all the ass photos with a boob shot. Or, even stranger, a picture of their toes. How weird was that? I supposed some guys had foot fetishes but would you focus your ad on that small market? It occurred to me I could write a guide to marketing for escorts.

I was getting nowhere.

The best way, I figured, was to search for her stage name. Jade. I went to backpage and typed her name in the little search area. Nothing. I went back to Google, and typed in Jade, then escort.

Several pages popped up, but they were a mixture of the same escort sites I'd seen before, plus some listings for custom jewelry. And most of the listings were for places all over the country, like Las Vegas and Los Angeles. A lot of women named Jade.

So I added Detroit to the search terms.

More results flooded my screen and I dutifully waded through them. So many of the photographs failed to show the woman's face. I understood that was on purpose. Some of these women probably had day jobs and were doing this on the side. The last thing they wanted would to be recognized.

After my eyes started to get dry and scratchy from staring at the screen I decided it was time to shut down the online search. Maybe there were better options somewhere else. I was about to shut the site down when I saw a listing at the bottom of the page for Platinum Escorts. There, I saw the word Jade attached to a thumbnail.

I clicked on the thumbnail.

A dark little thud landed on my stomach and the outlandishly pessimistic and cynical idea Nate suggested at dinner had just become a reality.

It was Kierra.

21

King of Breakfast, that's what I thought of myself. My alter ego. My superhero character. I was a morning person, no doubt about that, and I derived no greater pleasure than being the first one up, having my coffee, and making everyone breakfast.

The great thing about having young kids is that I was then able to immediately launch into making their lunches for school. King of Breakfast and Lunch. Which alleviated any guilt I had about not giving the slightest thought to dinners.

Although when Anna called me up and said she didn't have time to even think about dinner, I was always more than happy to either try to whip something up or order a meal and bring it home.

With the kids off to school, Anna's peck still fresh on my cheek, I headed out to the office.

The fact was, I was really trying to stay upbeat but the discovery that Kierra was possibly working as an escort did not sit well with me. While I had been home with my daughters, I had blocked the facts of the case and what I'd found. But now, on my way to work, I wondered what I should do.

My next meeting with Marvin Cotton wasn't really established. If suddenly he wanted to sit down and talk about what I'd found I would have no choice but to tell him. However, if I could put off meeting with him for awhile, maybe I could find out that it wasn't true. Or that she hadn't really been working as an escort. I wasn't holding out a ton of hope, but the strategy to buy some time seemed like a good one at the moment.

But I wasn't even a block from home when my cell phone rang from a number I didn't recognize.

"Hello?"

"John Rockne?"

"Speaking."

"This is Nix. We met when you came down to Destroy Records."

I thought I could hear the Hound from Hell in the background growling. He could probably hear my voice.

"Sure, I remember you, Mr. Nix."

"Not Mr. Nix. Just Nix." His tone had an edge to it. But when I pictured him in my mind I remembered that his entire being had an edge. The guy could cut you just walking past you in the grocery store.

I frowned at no one in particular.

"Okay, Nix."

"Grandmaster D would be more than happy to chat with you. He's playing basketball this morning at the Joe Dumars Fieldhouse in Detroit," he said. "Do you know where that is?"

It sounded like he was now lightly mocking me.

"Not offhand, no I don't," I said.

"It's off of Woodward at 8 Mile. Used to be the old state fairgrounds."

"Okay, I can be there in twenty minutes or so," I said, but instead of an answer I heard a dial tone.

"Goodbye and thank you, pal," I said to the dead line.

It actually took me a little more than twenty minutes to get to the Joe Dumars Fieldhouse as I hadn't anticipated the slight increase in traffic due to it being the tail end of rush hour.

As I drove down 8 Mile I passed Bush Gardens which, early in the morning, with an empty parking lot and all the lights shut off, had about as much charm and happiness as a used colostomy bag.

Eventually I saw an enormous sprawling field behind a barbed-wire fence. There were several large buildings, all boarded up with concrete barricades in front of the doors.

I spotted a narrow, weed-choked drive off of Woodward Avenue that led to the center of the buildings. There were about a dozen cars parked by a structure that had a row of windows near the top.

It was curious to me how the place had become associated with Joe Dumars, the ex-NBA basketball player. Why would he have purchased this place, I wondered. It looked like it should be condemned.

There was a spot near the entrance so I pulled up next to a Cadillac with Texas plates. Inside, I passed through a metal detector but the guy at the desk just waved me through.

The Fieldhouse was a collection of four full-length basketball courts all side-by-side. The walls near the entrance were covered with framed copies of vintage Sports Illustrated magazines. Each basketball court was occupied by guys playing hoops. All of them were black. I was the only white guy in the place.

I thought about joining a game but then remembered that I'm slow, out of shape, and can't shoot a basketball very well.

Instead, I went to the guy at the desk and asked if he could point out Grandmaster D for me. He looked at me with an expression somewhere between skepticism and hostility.

"Who the hell are you?"

Not a great demeanor for a front desk position. "He asked me to come and talk to him here. My name is John."

"Court 4," the man said. "The guy with the orange shoes."

"Thanks," I told him with very little enthusiasm. I walked down to Court 4 and sat in a miniature set of bleachers, only two rows high and watched the game.

It was mostly offense. In fact, half the guys didn't even run down the court to play defense. A lot of 3-point shots and the occasional dunk.

There was a woman in an energy drink T-shirt standing by a display. She looked bored.

Eventually, someone made a basket and half of the players threw their arms up in victory, and the other half walked off the court shaking their heads. The guy in the orange basketball shoes walked right up to me.

"You here to see me?" he asked.

He had on a gray T-shirt that was covered in sweat and he took a moment to chug from a bottle of Gatorade.

His skin was jet black and he had a diamond earring in each ear. They were big diamonds. Anna would be jealous, let's put it that way.

"Yeah, I'm John Rockne," I said. "Nix told me you would talk to me here."

It was kind of weird, so I decided to be up front. "So do I call you Grandmaster?"

He smiled. "Nah. My friends call me Derek."

"Okay. Derek. I wanted to ask you about Kierra Cotton. Sometimes she called herself Jade. I'm a private investigator and her Dad hired me to find her."

He nodded. "Yep, I knew Jade. Or Kierra. Whatever you want to call her."

He took a long drink from the bottle of Gatorade and looked at the woman standing off to our right.

"When did you see her last?" I asked.

Derek leaned back and looked at the Fieldhouse's rafters. "Probably a month or so ago. We used to party a little bit and she was really messed up. I let her stay at my place with some friends for a few days. I knew she was dabbling in the escort business and I told her that was a dead end."

Someone tossed him a towel and he wiped off his face. He threw his empty Gatorade bottle into a trash can at the foot of the bleachers and let out a small belch.

"Sorry," he said.

"No problem, my wife does that all the time."

He laughed and I said, "Ever hear of a company called Platinum Escorts?"

He shook his head, but I had a pretty good feeling he recognized the name. His nonchalance seemed practiced. A well-rehearsed move he did often. In his line of work, he probably had to lie to people all the time.

"What did Kierra say when you told her being an escort was a dead end?" I asked.

"Oh, the same thing everyone says," he said with a soft

laugh. "Don't matter if you're a thief or a drug dealer or a rapper. You know it's all going to end sooner than later, but you just want one more big score and then you swear you're going to get out once and for all. But you never do."

The guys on the court had started to reassemble and Derek looked over at them.

"That's what she said?" I asked. "She had a big score lined up?"

"Not exactly. But it sounded like she had a couple things going on that were going to let her get out. Man, if I had a dime for every time I heard that story."

"So that was it? You never saw her again?"

He shook his head. "Nope. She told someone she was going to work some auto convention or something and then she was gone."

Some of the players from the game were looking over at us.

"You want to join us?" Derek asked, nodding toward the court.

"No, I pulled a hammy cleaning my basement this weekend."

We shook hands and he said I could call him if I thought of any more questions. He produced one of his business cards and if his shorts didn't have pockets, I didn't want to think where it had come from. I also gave him one of my cards.

"I hope you find her," he added before he jogged back onto the court.

"I do, too," I said.

22

"**Y**ou white trash piece of shit."

AJ was dying and Clay was surprised. Even grudgingly respectful that the black punk could talk. He was cut in a hundred places and Clay thought he had bled out.

The 'white trash' comment made Clay think of a theory some bitch had told him in a bar. That Michigan's hillbillies were a particularly malignant form of redneck because during the great auto boom workers poured in from the south to Michigan to work in the car factories.

So, according to this woman, northern urban folks mingled with the true rednecks from the South to form some kind of hybrid mega white trash. Clay had laughed, then waited for the woman outside the bar and knocked all of her teeth out with a tire iron.

Clay looked at the black kid who knew he was dying and had decided to go out with an attempt at being a tough guy.

"What did you call me?" Clay asked.

The kid's bravado was fading fast. Clay could tell he wanted to cry. All these street punks were tough with their crews, their cell phones and knockoff Glocks. But take that shit away, make them face death, and they reverted to the scared little kids they really were.

"You heard me white boy," AJ said. His face was cracked and broken, he had cuts all over his body. He had lost a lot of blood.

Clay laughed. He thought again of that woman in the bar. Because he supposed there was some truth to the theory. Hell, his family had come from Kentucky to work at the Ford factory way back when. They'd sprawled out in some place called Centerline, a weird blue collar suburb of Detroit, and brought all of their Kentucky cousins and customs with them.

Eventually, when the jobs and money dried up, they'd gone slightly north, to the farm area where they'd turned to petty crime.

But they hadn't escaped the spread of racial unrest when the city of Detroit truly started to fall apart. As a kid, Clay had ended up being one of the few white kids left at his public school. He'd gotten singled out nearly every day. He learned to fight hard and fast and be more vicious than his opponents. If they had fists, he had a knife. If they had a knife, he had a gun.

And when he shot his first black punk, that was the end of school. His family had shipped him off with a crazy-ass uncle who stole things for a living.

First chance, he came back to the city.

And he had never forgotten his epic battles with the blacks.

"Did you call me white trash?" Clay said, his voice soft. He took off his leather jacket and set it on the back of a chair, well away from the action. He didn't want any blood to get on it.

"Goddamn right I did, asshole," the black guy said. "Fucking bitch."

Clay slashed him with the knife so fast it took a moment for his captive to realize he'd been stabbed. He jerked back, trying to avoid the blade but he was a full second too late. Clay had run the tip of the knife across the man's forehead, cutting loose a flap of skin that folded over on itself and looked like a unibrow made of meat. Blood poured into AJ's eyes and he yanked at his restraints.

With a laugh, Clay slashed the kid again, this time across the throat. A spray of blood shot from his neck and Clay stepped back, fascinated by the way the blood spurted in rhythmic pulses.

Clay was surprised yet again at how much blood had still been in the kid's body.

"When you call someone like me white trash, boy," Clay said, "you're not just insulting me, you're speaking badly of my kin going way back. And I don't take kindly to that. Especially from black garbage like you."

A groan escaped the young man and he slumped forward, no longer breathing.

"Get it?" Clay said. "White trash, black garbage?"

Clay wiped his blade clean on the kid's shirt.

"Yeah, I think you got it," he said.

23

T he first thing I did when I left the Joe Dumars Fieldhouse was to send Nate a text and ask him if he had ever heard of an escort service called Platinum Escorts.

When I swung into the village, I hit Starbucks and got myself a tall dark roast with some half and half and sugar. Anna wasn't around, because half and half and sugar in coffee were both against the house rules. We used fat free creamer and that was it. No added sugar.

But when the wife is away, even the most docile husband will play.

Back in my office armed with some delicious caffeine, I scoured the Internet for Platinum Escorts. And not their lame-ass website full of shots of girls. Because there was nothing at all on the website other than those images and an email address that I'm sure was not going to be easy to track down.

When I searched from a business address perspective, there were a ton of them, and that was the problem. There was Platinum Escorts, Las Vegas. Platinum Escorts, New York. Los Angeles. Dallas. Miami.

That's a lot of platinum.

Nothing in Detroit, though.

It was a safe guess that these kinds of companies had a million different names for themselves. After all, most of the photos used for one "service" were the same photos for another one. Once they had enough photos, they probably just plastered them all over the Internet with different email addresses or phone numbers that most likely led to the same answering service or whatever scam system they used.

Despite what most people think, looking at photos of scantily clad women, especially young scantily clad women, can get tiresome. Especially when you consider the widespread practice of human trafficking, of which there was quite a bit in the Midwest, and Detroit in particular.

It felt great to close the browser and step away from the computer.

There hadn't been much hope that I would be able to get an address or a name from the Web. These kinds of companies were evading law enforcement. But I hadn't even found anything about Platinum Escorts in any other location. Like police reports. Or news stories.

The fact was, you could only do so much research online. The world was still a place inhabited by people made of flesh and blood, not constructed of electronic pulses and pixels.

So I decided to change gears.

I gambled that Nate might be able to point to someone who could help with the Platinum Escort angle.

That meant I could focus on the auto convention Derek had told me about, when he said that Jade was hoping for a big score so she could get out of the business.

So what auto convention? And where? And who would Kierra have been there with?

The good news was that you couldn't live in Detroit without knowing a lot of people in the auto industry. And I mean a lot. The people who weren't actually in the industry itself, in other words, working directly for Ford, GM or Chrysler, were usually working at industries that supported the auto manufacturers. Plastics suppliers. Leather suppliers. Gadgets and gizmos. Nuts and bolts. Someone had to make all of the million little pieces that the auto factories farmed out.

Now, I thought long and hard about who I could call that would have the best information when it came to auto conventions.

The name came immediately to me. Her name was Donna and she was a friend of Anna's. I'd met her a bunch of times at various parties and knew she was a bigwig at Ford, alongside one of the famous Fords, but also heavily involved in marketing. She would know all about conventions.

I called Anna and asked her for Donna's number.

"Why do you want it?" she asked.

"Oh, she's been hitting on me for years and I finally decided to give in."

"She's a lucky girl," Anna said, then gave me the number. "Tell her I said hi," she added.

I've always been pleased that my wife and I are secure in our relationship, but sometimes I wished she'd at least *pretend* that another woman might be interested in me.

Since Donna's job sounded high-powered and super important, I figured she was a very busy woman. And I guessed that I wouldn't get her the first time I tried her number.

But I was wrong.

After an exchange of pleasantries, I asked her about auto conventions. Like, how many are there, where are they, and were there any recently.

"Are you kidding me, John?" she asked.

"No."

"Conventions are to car guys like Fort Lauderdale is to spring breakers," Donna said. "They find any and all excuses to have them. And they're ridiculous."

"Ridiculous how?"

"These guys go and the companies like Ford set up displays of the latest vehicles and technology and there are usually some reporters around," she patiently explained. "But then at around three o'clock in the afternoon, although I swear, it gets earlier the longer I'm in this business, they roll out the bars."

"Mobile bars?" I asked. I liked the sound of that. Maybe I would get one for my office.

"Yep. Complete with bartenders and usually some pretty girls around."

Pretty girls.

"So were there any recently?" I asked.

"There were three last weekend. The biggest one being in Los Angeles."

I thought back to Kierra's social media accounts. It wasn't last weekend. I ran through some quick timing scenarios.

"It probably would have been around three or four weekends ago, and I don't think it would have been too far away, like New York or L.A."

"Traverse City, I bet," Donna said. "There was a convention in Traverse City in that time frame, one of the big ones.

All of the players would have been there. May I ask why you're so curious?"

"I'm working on a missing persons case," I said. "An auto convention might have been one of the last places she was seen."

"Is she one of those pretty girls I was just talking about?"

Either women are extremely perceptive or I'm just a friggin' open book.

"I'm afraid so," I admitted. "So what was in Traverse City?"

"North American Automobile Technology Expo," she said. "Not so much for the gear heads, but with the way the industry is going, this has already gotten to be as big as all of the other ones."

"So when was it? And did you go?"

"No, I didn't go," she laughed, her tone rueful. "Thank God. It was three weekends ago. Just go online, I'm sure you can find all of the details still on the website. They might even have pictures from the event."

Just to be sure, I had her run down any other big auto shows that had happened within the past month or so, but I had a feeling the one in Traverse City was the one I needed to investigate.

"Tell Anna I said hello," she said. I promised I would and thanked her.

"My pleasure, John. You know, I hope I didn't make it sound like it was some kind of horrible debauchery. Most of the guys are usually harmless and just looking for an excuse to get plastered. I really doubt any harm would have come to your missing girl at the convention."

I thought about that and wasn't sure I agreed.

But just to be pleasant I said, "You're probably right. At least I hope so."

24

W hen you ask someone from Michigan where they live, or where their vacation cottage is, or where they're from, they'll inevitably hold up their hand, palm facing away, to represent the "mitten" shape that is the state. They'll then point to an exact location on their hand.

If you were to do this with Traverse City, it would be on the left side of the mitten, near the top of the pinky.

The area was home to a lot of picturesque little towns where some of the wealthier Detroit suburbanites got away during the summer. Petoskey, Harbor Springs and other towns near Traverse City were the hub of these warm weather activities, mostly because of the lakes.

That part of Michigan was home to not only spectacular Lake Michigan shoreline, but dozens of beautiful inland lakes, some of them spring-fed and almost Caribbean in beauty.

Traverse City was the biggest of the towns and it even had a fairly good-sized airport. Most of the flights went directly into Detroit for connections, but it saved folks four and half hours in the car, and that's on good days. On Sundays, the freeway, I-75, was choked with traffic coming back "down" from their cottages.

Not necessarily wanting to hop in the car and make the drive, I decided to see if I could find any news of the convention online. Reluctantly, I powered the computer back up, logged in and started searching around for news of the event. NAATE. North American Automobile Technology Expo.

Sounded fascinating.

If it were me, I would spend about a half hour at the convention and then sneak out and go to the beach.

It didn't take long for me to find the website for the event, but it was nothing more than the schedule with links to nearby hotels and restaurants.

Still, I printed off the schedule as it had a list of some names and speakers.

I found a Traverse City news website but after digging through their entertainment section I still came up blank. Not a lot of entertainment going on in Traverse City, other than a country music act I'd never heard of and a fishing derby. Such a strange name. I pictured human-sized salmon on roller skates trying to knock each other over.

My luck changed when I stumbled across a local blogger who had been at the convention and taken some photos.

There were only a handful of pictures but I could see that the convention had been a much bigger deal than I thought. It looked like there was a large dining hall and at least several hundred people were there.

I sent an email to the blogger through a form on the site, and then made the executive decision to drive to Traverse City to interview the staff at the hotel. There was no way I could do it from Grosse Pointe. And from experience I knew that calling the hotel and asking for information about the guests would get me nowhere. Hotel staff were notoriously tight-lipped when it came to their guests and most of them knew they would get fired for giving out the wrong information to the wrong people.

I made sure to grab my little mileage notebook so I could write the trip off.

With a brief stop at home to throw a change of clothes into a duffel bag and a quick goodbye to the family, I headed out on I-75 and figured I could make it to the site of the convention before they closed and everyone who was anyone went home.

It began to rain by the time I passed Auburn Hills and when I was passing the Birch Run outlet mall it was coming down in sheets.

If it hadn't been for the rain, I would have appreciated noticing the change in geography one experiences when heading to the northwest of Michigan's lower peninsula. For much of the drive, the scenery is flat farmland. But the chunks of glaciers that created so many lakes in the area also left some beautiful bluffs and rolling hills.

When I hit the first of those big rises I knew I was getting close to Traverse City. As if on cue, the rain shut down and I rolled into town at the same time I was finally able to shut off the windshield wipers.

My navigation app directed me to the Traverse City Hilton, which had a nice spot overlooking a beautiful stretch of Lake Michigan.

I parked, went inside and asked to speak to the manager. It was only 4:30 so I figured he or she hadn't left for the day.

As luck would have it, she was still in and available to chat.

Her name was Marcy Conklin and she was a solid-looking woman with curly red hair and puffy cheeks.

After introductions were made, she invited me back to her office and asked me, "What can we do for you, Mr. Rockne?"

I sat down in a pleather chair across from her, noticed the mounted fish on the wall.

"Lake Trout," she said, following my eyes. "My husband is a charter fisherman."

"Nice," I said. "I'm here following a lead on a missing girl."

Her eyes went a little wide.

"What, was she a guest here?" she asked. I could see a slight sense of panic in her eyes. Not that she was guilty of anything, but I remembered that Traverse City was a small town, and they didn't get as much crime as Detroit.

"I don't believe she was a registered guest, but is there any way you can check?"

"Sure, I can't give out certain kinds of information but I can tell you if we had a reservation under that name."

I gave her Kierra's name and Marcy clicked away on the computer, shook her head and her curls gave little jiggles.

"No, sir, no sign of that guest," she said and I could hear the relief in her voice.

Well, I knew Kierra wouldn't have booked a room under Jade, and if she was working the event, she probably would have been with a client.

It would be overstepping my bounds to ask for a guest list and even though Marcy seemed an apple-pie-small-town kind of gal, I knew she wouldn't go for that.

"Did you have anyone taking pictures during the convention?" I asked.

"We didn't, but I believe there was a photographer

present," she said. "I seem to recall people posing for photographs when the awards were handed out."

"Awards?"

"Oh, they gave an award or two for people who contributed to some charities, I believe."

"How would I find out who that photographer was?" I asked.

"Ralph would know," she said. "He's my assistant manager and he took care of any media requests. Hold on, I'll see if he's in."

She picked up the phone and I took another glance at the big lake trout on the wall. That had to be tough to handle, glued to a piece of wood and forced to look out at the lake you once swam in.

"Hi Ralph, what was the name of the photographer who handled the auto convention?" Marcy said into the phone. She waited and then jotted something down on a notepad. "Thank you, and don't forget to contact the parents of those fraternity boys who pooped in the elevator."

Marcy hung up, and her face flushed a little.

"Boys will be boys," I said.

"Harris Photography was in charge of pictures, they have a studio down on Main Street." She glanced at the clock.

"You can probably catch them before they close up shop for the night."

"Okay, I'll try to do that," I said. "Thank you, Marcy. I may come back if I have to spend the night."

She handed me a business card.

"I'll see to it you get the best room in the hotel," she said, with a little wink.

From the time I left Marcy's office to the time I opened the front door to Harris Photography a whole five minutes had elapsed. Say what you will about small town America, it had its perks.

There was no one in the shop, which consisted of one small room whose walls were adorned floor-to-ceiling with photographs. A glass case sat at the back. Behind it stood a door that was only partially open.

"Hello?" I said as I walked toward the back of the room, hundreds of sets of eyes from high school graduation photos following my every room. An incredibly large canvas featuring an Italian Greyhound dressed in a cardigan sweater caught my eye. Some people *really* loved their pets.

I heard someone curse under their breath and then a thin man with a porn mustache peeked out at me from behind the door.

"Was just about to leave," he said, very little attempt to conceal the annoyance in his voice.

"Oh, sorry about that," I said. "I was wondering if I could take a look at the photographs you shot at the auto convention a few weekends back."

He stood up and I was shocked at how tall he was. Easily 6'8" or 6'9".

"Yeah, I don't have time to show them to you," he said. "If you come back–"

"I'll pay you for them. Fifty bucks for everything you shot."

I had to be bold because this guy obviously had a hot date. Hopefully she was a volleyball player or a walking pituitary gland.

"Cash?" he asked.

Stretch was way too young to own the place, so I smelled an under-the-table kind of deal.

"Of course," I said, congratulating myself for having the

foresight to withdraw some cash before I'd left Grosse Pointe.

"Okay, hold on," he said.

I heard him tap away on a computer followed by a couple of clips and snaps. A minute or two later he handed me a thumb drive and I gave him the money.

"They're all on there," he said. "Probably about five hundred shots or so. Hi-res. Boring as hell. Don't know why anyone would want them."

"It was a big event for me, I was honored as Wiper Blade Supplier of the Year," I said. "I could really use some more pictures for my scrapbook."

He shook his head as if to say, 'whatever.'

Lurch walked me out of the office then and he shut and locked the door behind me.

Unfortunately, I had more than enough time to make it back to Grosse Pointe at a reasonable hour so I wouldn't be needing the nicest room at the Traverse City Hilton.

Oh, well. Something told me it would pretty much always be available if I ever needed it.

25

When I made it home, the girls were in bed, but the better half was still up. She was sprawled out on the couch in our family room, eyes half-mast, a nature show on the television.

I went upstairs, changed into a T-shirt and shorts, grabbed the iPad from our home office and went into the family room. I transferred the photos from the thumb drive to the computer and then put them on the iPad. I joined Anna on the couch.

"What you got there?" Anna said. "Did you really go to Traverse City and back today?"

"Yep."

"Hope you kept track of the mileage," she said.

"Sure did, dear," I said. As I watched the progress bar of the photo app on the iPad continue to process the pictures I stood back up. "Want a drink?"

"Sure, why not?" she said. I grabbed a beer from the fridge for me, dumped some white wine in a glass for Anna and dropped in an ice cube – just the way she liked it.

When I got back, she was sitting up on the couch, with her feet up on the ottoman and the television turned off.

We clinked, and I sat down next to her, put the iPad between us.

"Want to look at some dirty pictures with me?" I asked.

"Are they of us?"

"You wish," I said. "You love to see me in action. From every possible angle."

"That's true," Anna said. "I was just watching that nature show about lowland gorillas. Totally made me think of you."

"Hey, I'm no lowlander, I'm an uplander gorilla. Isn't that a Billy Joel song?"

"Uptown Girl," Anna said. "I hate that song."

"Christie Brinkley was good in it, though."

"That's the video, not the song."

"Aren't they the same?" I asked. Anna rolled her eyes.

The photos finished loading and the first one popped up on the iPad's screen. I changed the setting so all of the images would go full screen and I could just slide them with a finger swipe.

"There's a lot," I warned my wife. "You might get bored."

"That's okay, occupational hazard."

I wasn't sure if she meant my occupation, or hers.

The first photo was of a few guys standing around a car whose dashboard had been pulled apart to expose the wiring and gizmos inside.

"Look at that guy's suit," Anna said. "Was this a convention or a costume party?"

"Please, we're looking for Kierra," I said. "But that guy's suit is bad. It looks like velvet."

I swiped and then swiped again. And again. And again.

Gradually, the photos began to change from people

standing around cars to people standing around drinking alcohol.

"It looks like everyone was pounding the booze," Anna said. "And I'm not surprised. That party looks like about as much fun as an infected toenail."

It did look painfully boring. One of the pictures was of a band that answered the eternal question of whatever happened to the Lawrence Welk musicians.

"Should be easy to spot her, if you know what I mean," my wife pointed out. I *did* know what she meant. There weren't many African-Americans at the party.

The swiping continued with no avail.

"Are you sure she was there?" Anna asked.

"Not exactly sure, but I think she was." I explained a little about meeting Grandmaster D and what he said.

"I suppose you want me to call you Grandmaster of something," Anna said.

"Hmm, I hadn't thought of that, but now that you mention it," I said. Actually I had thought of it.

Grandmaster of Love.

"Grandmaster of Love, I bet," my wife said, reminding me again that I should never try to put something past her. It would never work.

"There!" I practically shouted.

"Shhh, you'll wake the girls," she said.

It was a perfect profile shot of Kierra, or Jade, as she was probably calling herself during this shindig.

"Wow, she looks so different from that other photo you showed me," Anna said.

And she did. Lots of makeup. A tight black dress that showed off an amazing figure. She'd lost weight.

"And so much older."

She was looking up at a man who had his back to the

camera. He was tall, with a fine mane of silver hair. The suit he wore looked expensive.

I held my finger on the photo until the toolbar appeared and I sent the image to myself via email.

Then I let go and swiped again.

The hope that it would be a string of photos of Kierra vanished. The next shot was a different setting altogether. I went through the rest of all the photos and that was the only one.

"Well, one out of five hundred," I said.

"Now what are you going to do?" Anna asked.

I took a long drink of my beer, reopened my email and forwarded the message I'd sent myself to Harris Photography, Marcy, and the Traverse City blogger, asking all three of them if they knew who the man with the silver hair was and if they had any other pictures of the girl.

Once it sent, I ejected the thumb drive and powered the iPad down, and finished my beer.

"What am I going to do?" I repeated. "I'm going to take you upstairs and show you why they call me the Grandmaster."

26

The mail at the office consisted of glossy catalogs from a local jewelry store and a women's western wear company. Had someone put me on a mailing list for a joke? I filed them in the wastebasket, sat at my desk and pulled out my phone.

The first message went to Nate and I included a photo of Kierra at the auto convention with the silver-haired man. I asked him if he had any idea who the guy might be, even though you couldn't really see his face. There were a few people in the background of the shot and I thought maybe Nate would recognize a face or two.

It was free and worth a shot.

Next up was my weekly check of the bank account. It was okay news. A few deposits had finally landed for some divorce work I'd done a few months back. My automatic deductions for rent and Internet service had cleared.

All in all, I was doing fine.

But I hadn't charged Marvin Cotton a high rate and I'd been spending a fair amount of time on the case. So I typed up an estimate for the invoice thus far and emailed it to him.

While my email was open, I answered several prospective client questions. One asking if I handled business espionage cases, to which I responded in the affirmative. Of course I did. Just about every question I received that asked if I had experience in a certain field was answered in the affirmative. I wasn't lying. So much of what I did crossed a lot of lines. In every sense.

The second email asked if I handled prospective divorce cases, to which I also responded positively. The "prospective" divorce case question always meant a spouse suspected the other of cheating. Always.

Speaking of cheating, my mind went back to Kierra and the escort service. She used the name Jade. I assumed her clients all used fake names, too. But how did they pay? Cash, most likely. But I knew there were some high profile cases where politicians used their credit cards. Which was incredibly stupid.

Same thing in the case of some website for affairs that had been invaded by Russian hackers and the database posted publicly. Hopeful cheaters had supplied the website with their real names, addresses, phone numbers and credit card information. You have to be pretty horny or pretty dumb to do that. Maybe a little bit of both.

It made me wonder how and who took Kierra to the auto convention. Did a client pay for her travel? For her services the whole time she was up there? Or was it the escort service, Platinum Escorts, that sent her up there and told her to service some clients?

And then I realized what I'd missed. I swung my feet off the desk and sat up straight. Grabbed my phone.

Derek had told me that Kierra was thinking of leaving the escort business. That she'd had a couple of big scores lined up and was going to try to leave after that. The auto convention was the one she'd told him about.

What was the other one?

Obviously, he hadn't told me for a reason. And I had assumed it was because he didn't know. But what if he did?

In my wallet was the card he'd given me with his number. So I punched it in, half expecting it wasn't really his number.

But he answered on the second ring.

"Yeah?"

"Derek, it's John Rockne, the private investigator looking into the Kierra Cotton case."

"Yeah." He sounded less than enthused to be talking to me again.

"Listen, you told me that Kierra said she had a couple of big gigs lined up and then she was going to try to get out of the escort business. One of them was the auto convention. Do you know what the other one was?"

There was a slight pause and then he said, "Naw, man. She only said something about that auto thing."

"Nothing at all about the other one? When it was. Or where it might be?" I asked. That pause in his answer suggested that he might not be telling me everything. But why would he lie now? He'd obviously been telling the truth about the auto convention.

"Sorry, man, I told you what I knew."

I let the silence hang for awhile. It sounded like a lie, maybe even to him.

"Okay, well call me if you think of anything. Anything at all," I said.

He didn't answer because he'd already disconnected.

I was staring at the phone as I watched Nate's name and number appear on my screen. I slid the answer button.

"Hey," I said.

"How am I supposed to recognize people from the back of their heads?" he asked.

"It's a new investigative technique," I answered. "Rear cranial identification approaches. It's all the rage in law enforcement these days."

"Very funny," he said without a stitch of humor in his voice. "Oddly enough, I might know who it is."

"You're kidding me," I said. I grabbed a notepad and a pen. "Shoot."

"I think he's an attorney."

I jotted down "attorney" on the notepad.

And waited.

Finally, I said, "That's it?"

"Yeah."

"That's not saying *who* it is. That's saying *what* he is."

"I know, I know. But I think I can figure it out. Not on an empty stomach, though."

I rolled my eyes.

"Have you heard about that new crepe place?" Nate asked. "Let's meet there tomorrow. I might have an answer for you."

I sighed into the phone.

"Okay."

27

C lay Hitchfield loved a good titty bar. He wished there were more titty places of business. Titty grocery stores. Titty gas stations.

The titty bar by the airport was mostly empty except for a skinny dancer on stage, a bartender and two businessmen sitting together at the foot of the stage, occasionally putting a dollar bill in the skinny girl's underwear and slapping her ass.

Clay waited for his eyes to adjust and then spotted the other guest of The Runway. It was John Wayne, a.k.a. his employer, a.k.a. the big guy with the fine head of silver hair, sitting in a booth at the back of the place. The worst seat in the house to see the dancers, but the best seat if you didn't want to be noticed.

He wanted to laugh. The guy *really* didn't want to be seen with him.

Clay walked up to the bar, ordered a beer and pointed to the guy in the booth, telling the bartender to put it on that guy's tab.

Then Clay joined his meal ticket in the booth.

"Enjoying the show?" Clay asked.

John Wayne took a sip from his drink. It looked like Scotch. On the rocks.

"I need an update," the man said. Clay noticed his fancy suit, his big watch, the way he looked around the place like he was worried about germs.

Clay smiled and took a drink of his beer. "The black kid was a dead end. Literally."

He laughed, picturing how he'd dumped the kid's body into the cistern full of acid.

"Great," the man said. He shook his glass from side to side, let the ice mix with the remnants of the liquor and then drank. The expression on his face wasn't so much disappointment as resignation. As if he had known all along that Clay wouldn't come through for him.

"Hey, it's not my fault the asshole didn't know anything," Clay said. "You were wrong. Your information was bad. That hood rat had no idea where the girl was. Believe me, he would have coughed it up, considering the pain he was in."

The chick on the bar was on her hands and knees, her ass in the face of one of the business guys. Clay felt himself get hard. It'd been awhile since he'd had a woman. If he could get some cash from his client here, maybe he'd make an offer to the skinny bitch for a quickie somewhere. Maybe she'd let him rough her up a little bit. Or, more likely, he'd do it anyway, with or without her consent.

Old Silver Hair reached into his sport coat and pulled out a couple sheets of paper and a photograph.

It was a shot of some middle-aged guy.

"This guy's a private investigator," he said. "Name is John Rockne. He was hired by the girl's father to try to find her. We think he's making some progress."

"Who's we?"

The man ignored him.

"Follow him. See what he's looking into. If you have to, get the information from him. He's got an office in Grosse Pointe. You know where that is?"

Clay shook his head. "No, but I've heard of it. That's where all the rich fucks live, right?"

The guy ignored his question again. Clay was starting to get a little pissed. He hated being ignored.

"You have to be really careful with this guy, though," Silver Hair said. "His sister is Chief of Police of Grosse Pointe. Anything happens to him, you're going to have cops all over your ass."

"So, what are you telling me? Don't touch him?" Clay almost laughed at the idea. That wasn't the way he worked. He wasn't what you would call…an observer. He liked to get his hands dirty. Or better yet, bloody.

"I didn't say that," the man said. "I simply pointed out that if you touch him, you're going to have cops all over your ass. So either don't do it, or if you do, be smart about it."

The guy smirked when he said that, and Clay knew it was about the idea of him being smart. The bastard thought it was funny.

"If you do it, don't get caught," Silver Hair said. "And if you get caught, keep your fucking mouth shut. Got it?"

Clay's eyes drifted to the guy's watch. It wasn't overly gaudy, but he could see the name Patek Philippe.

That sounded expensive to Clay.

It would be a two-step process. Stick a knife into John Wayne's chest. Steal watch.

Now it was his time to smirk.

He scooped up the papers and the photograph.

"I need my next installment," he said.

John Wayne got to his feet and dropped an envelope onto the table.

"Find her, or that's the last of it," he said.

Clay laughed as the man walked away.

I'll decide when it's the end of it, he thought.

28

I t was time to get the ears lowered and I had a strict philosophy when it came to haircuts. I wanted the dollar amount to equal the minutes required to do the job. And in both cases, the lower the better. In other words, a ten-dollar haircut that took ten minutes was ideal. Even better? A nine-dollar haircut that took nine minutes. You get the idea.

I went to this fancy, French-inspired salon called Cheap Cuts. Yes, I'm kidding. Nothing French, or salon-looking. Cheap Cuts was my kind of place.

There was a five-minute wait so I took a seat and picked up the newspaper someone had left on the table next to a well-worn Good Housekeeping. Did they still publish Good Housekeeping? Who read that anymore? I remember my Mom reading that magazine. Surely the publication's audience now spent most of their reading time on prescription labels at the old folks home.

There was the usual blather about the Detroit sports teams, and on the politics page a shot of the Mayor.

Detroit's Mayor was a man named Bill Mahorn, a former professional basketball player who had never been a star player, but a journeyman who had endeared himself to the city's populace by being one of those blue-collar, hard-working kind of guys.

He was an African-American but also well-liked by Detroit's mostly white suburbs, not that it mattered in terms of getting elected. Suburbanites don't get a vote in Detroit, but it helps if the candidate looks like he or she can work with people outside of the city.

Despite his workmanlike reputation on the basketball court, he had always been rumored to have a playboy-like mentality off the court. A large entourage followed him everywhere and there were rumors that he had multiple children with multiple women pretty much all over the country.

Now, on this report in the newspaper, he was surrounded by that entourage as he discussed more attempts to get funding from the state government in Lansing for some of the city's floundering projects. It was a never-ending request, time worn by all of the previous administrations.

I was about to flip the page and go to the entertainment section of the paper when something made me stop.

The photograph was intriguing.

There was big Mahorn, standing head and shoulders above everyone else, flanked by his security team.

None of the faces looked familiar to me.

Except one.

It was Nix.

The guy at Destroy Records who had asked me why I wanted to talk with Grandmaster D.

He worked for the Mayor, too?

That seemed odd to me.

And why had the photo jumped out at me?

The Detroit community was a small one. It made perfect sense that some of the Mayor's entourage might also have ties with one of the city's most famous musicians.

In fact, Mahorn had sometimes referred to himself as America's first hip-hop mayor.

A weird feeling ran down my back. I actually started sweating.

My iPad. It was at the office. I got up and walked out of Cheap Cuts, got into the car and drove immediately back to my office, ran up my steps and barged into my office. I grabbed the iPad and started at the beginning. I already knew that what I was looking for wasn't in the photograph of Kierra.

But I wondered, had I seen Nix in the auto convention photos?

I remembered Anna and I joking about the fact that it would be easy to see Kierra because there were so few African-Americans at the convention. But there had been a few. One in particular I now remembered.

The photos flew past me until I got to the one I was looking for. It was a shot of the band and off to one side, standing at a table partially obscured by two other people, was a black man. Most of his body was blocked from view, but I could just make out the side of his face. I used my fingers to enlarge the photo.

Damn, it was entirely possible that the man in the photo was Nix. It had to be. He had that angular face, with a sharp nose. The man had a presence. Even in this crappy photo.

I made a copy of the photo, then cropped it so Nix's face

filled the screen. It was a little pixelated but my gut told me it was him.

And for the first time, I had a really bad feeling about what had happened to Kierra.

29

U nfortunately, I didn't know anyone at the mayor's office, and I couldn't even think of anyone who might have a contact there.

So I tried a cold call.

The first person I spoke with immediately transferred me to the head of public relations and I left a message saying I had some questions for the mayor's security team regarding the case of a missing girl.

It seemed like a good bet that I would never hear back from anyone.

There was also a fairly good risk I was going to wear out my welcome with Grandmaster D, but until Nix was ready to talk to me directly, he was the only source I had for more information about him.

I called the cell phone number and this time he didn't answer. Instead of leaving a message on his voicemail I took a chance and sent him a text message asking him if we could again meet face to face.

When he called me a few minutes later, he gave me an address in downtown Detroit. He said it was his recording studio and that they would be there well into the evening. It sounded like he would be willing to speak with me when they took a break.

There was a moment when I thought how cool it would be if I could rap a few lyrics onto one of Grandmaster D's songs. Yeah, probably not.

With that dream quashed, I figured there was no better time than the present so I punched in the address on my phone and followed the directions down to a place right off of Jefferson, to a warehouse district that ran along the banks of the Detroit River.

These buildings had been boarded up for as long as I could remember. There used to be a great blues bar in the area that I had frequented years ago, but that was gone, too. It was difficult to find the place because there were no street signs and none of the buildings had any address numbers anywhere to be found.

My first inkling I was close, though, was when I came across a Bentley coupe parked next to a Mercedes G-Wagon parked next to an Aston Martin.

My minivan looked cooler than all of them, so I parked a block away, not wanting to outshine them so obviously.

I walked back and found the main entrance, but it was locked.

There was no doorbell and no speaker.

A quick look around showed a couple of vacant lots, some bits of broken glass on the street and in the background, the Renaissance Center and the skyline of Detroit. The RenCen as it was called was home to General Motors headquarters.

It made me a little nervous to do it, but I reached up and pounded on the door and then I waited.

After fifteen minutes of waiting, I texted Derek's cell phone and told him I was outside.

I waited another thirty minutes and pounded on the door again.

It occurred to me that maybe it was a wild goose chase. Bring pesky guy down and then make him stand outside until he gives up. I was less than ten minutes from home, I could drive back and have dinner with the family.

But someone was here.

These hundred thousand dollar cars didn't drive themselves down here. Then again, maybe they did. They probably talked about it at the automotive technology expo in Traverse City.

The door opened behind me.

A huge, hulking guy looked down at me. He was bald, with a thick beard, and massive arms covered in tattoos.

He appraised me like I was a sprawling patch of crabgrass invading his lawn.

"No need to pound on the door, man." He raised his chin and for the first time I noticed the small camera pointed down at the door.

"Oh, sorry," I said. "I was hoping to talk to Grandmaster D."

"He'll be out in a few minutes," the giant said. "Why don't you do some push ups while you wait for him."

"Um–"

"Like, why don't you give me twenty." He said it as a statement, not a question.

Was I really just being told to drop and give him twenty?

I started looking around for a patch of clear grass or pavement.

"I'm just fucking with you, man," he said. He smiled, and his teeth were covered with gold caps.

He stepped aside and Derek walked out, a cloud of marijuana smoke following him. The door slammed shut behind him.

"Hey, I've only got a minute or so," he said.

"What can you tell me about Nix?" I said.

Derek's eyes were a little bloodshot and I could smell booze on him.

"What about him?"

"Well, does he work for you?"

Derek smiled. "Nix works for Nix, man."

"Oh, I was under the impression–"

"Does this really have something to do with Jade?" he asked. Derek was higher than a drone flown by a neighborhood Dad.

"Yes," I answered. "I think Nix was at the auto convention where Jade was working." I pulled out my phone and showed him the picture of Jade, and then the picture of Nix that I had cropped and sent to Nate.

Derek shrugged his shoulders.

"I don't know anything about that, man."

I sensed the same reluctance I'd heard before when I asked about the second big score Kierra had mentioned.

"Are you scared of him?" I said. "Of Nix?"

It sort of slipped out, and I worried it was the wrong thing to say, but Derek just laughed. "If you've got any kind of sense, you're scared of Nix. The man plays for keeps, do you know what I mean?"

"So he doesn't work for you," I said. "Does he work for the mayor?"

The door cracked open, and Hulk said, "They're ready for you."

The door shut again.

Derek looked at me. "Look, I really wanted to help you,

because I think Jade, or Kierra, is a good kid. But I don't know what happened to her. And if you start rattling Nix's cage, you better be careful."

He took a step away from me.

"Here's what I'm going to tell you and then I'm not going to answer any more of your calls or have any more conversations about this," he said.

He took a deep breath and I was glad he was a little high, because I don't think I would have gotten this out of him sober.

"Nix is like a freelance security guy," he said. "Mostly unofficial. But he's been keeping a pretty low profile since that big party they had a couple weeks ago."

"Party?"

Derek smiled. "Man, don't you read the papers? That big party at the Mansion?"

A big party? I frowned trying to remember if I'd heard anything. Maybe I had.

"That's all I got," Derek said. "Don't bother me anymore. We square?"

I started to answer but then the door opened, Derek nodded at me, and he disappeared inside. The Hulk stood looking at me for a minute, and then I walked away.

I heard the door slam shut behind me.

30

The restaurant was called The Crepe Escape and it was a new addition to the part of Grosse Pointe at the end of Kercheval where it hit Alter Road. The village had gotten into trouble because at some point someone had the idea to just shut the road off right there, so they dragged some big pots and shit across it.

Naturally, this didn't sit well with the Detroiters across the street, so Grosse Pointe business owners opened Kercheval back up and made a nice little circular drive.

Nate and I got there at the same time and since it was an order-at-the-counter kind of place, I went first to give the big man time to study the menu.

He didn't like to be rushed.

I ordered a Nutella crepe because when I looked at the menu, the name Nutella jumped out at me. I love Nutella. I want to find Nutella headquarters and apply for a job there so I can get free Nutella.

Nate finally made up his mind and ordered three crepes, all of them having nothing to do with breakfast, which is what I thought a crepe was meant for. His had meat in them.

And not breakfast meat like bacon. Chicken, beef and something else.

We sat down and I got a coffee. Nate ordered a Coke.

He slid a piece of paper across the table.

"That's the info I could find on Platinum Escorts," he said. "I talked to a buddy who knows a buddy who works Vice in Detroit. Apparently this group is on their radar. But since it's strictly high-end and they're supposedly not into the really bad stuff like kidnapping, they're pretty much left alone. For now."

I glanced at the name and the address.

"You're kidding me," I said. "Birmingham?"

Birmingham was a fancy little suburb north of Detroit at Woodward and Maple Road. A lot of wealthy people lived in Birmingham, along with its neighbor Bloomfield Hills. I'd just had a case take me to Birmingham not too long ago.

"There's no such thing as cheap rent in Birmingham," Nate said. "So either they own the building, or they're making a lot of money and can afford the rent."

"Who is Argyle?" I asked. That was the only name on the paper, next to the address.

"No idea, John," Nate said.

He looked tired. No one would ever accuse him of being a snazzy dresser and currently his shirt was wrinkled and untucked, his jeans looked like they hadn't seen a washing machine for awhile and his hair was sticking like he'd been electrocuted.

I folded up the piece of paper and put it in my pocket as our food came.

The freaking Nutella was delicious. For once, I finished my meal faster than Nate.

While he ate, I told him about Nix, my meeting with Derek and my request to talk to Mayor Bill Mahorn.

"Horny Mahorn?" he said. "Mayor Mahorny?"

I hadn't heard those nicknames. "I have to get out more," I said, shaking my head. "That's what they really call him?"

Nate raised an eyebrow. "Some do. His enemies, probably."

"Well, that makes sense if there was some crazy party a few weeks back," I said. "Did you hear anything about that?"

"Sure. At the mayor's mansion. It got out of hand, a couple of fights broke out, the cops had to come and stop it. Not a good public relations move."

"Since they call him Mayor Mahorny, I'm guessing there were a lot of women at this party," I pointed out. "Maybe even a few paid to be there?"

"Of course," Nate said, spearing a huge chunk of crepe that was dripping with spinach and melted mozzarella. "The mayor throws a big party, invites some of his big fundraisers, you're damn right he's got women there. Probably assigned to certain big contributors to the mayor's war chest."

I drained the rest of my coffee.

"I know one of the cops who worked the party that night," Nate said. He dug out his cell phone, worked the screen for a bit and then I saw a contact in my text messages.

"Give him a call, he's a young guy, son of the sports editor. He'll be able to tell you more. I don't know anything else about it."

He looked at me. "Are you thinking your missing girl was at the party?"

"It's just a guess but the timeline fits."

A thought occurred to me. "So every mayor has his own legal team, right?"

"Well, private attorneys, sure," Nate said after considering the question. "Whether or not they've got some on the public payroll, I'm not sure."

"You said you thought the guy with the silver hair might have been an attorney, right?"

"Yeah, but it was just a guess. I can't tell anything from the back of the guy's head."

It was a glimmer of an idea but I had nothing to back it up. There were a million attorneys in the city. But Nix had been at the auto convention. Jade had been there, too.

What I really needed to do was figure out if Jade had been at the mayor's party, and if the guy with the silver hair had been there, too.

Maybe the answer was in Birmingham.

31

The drive to Birmingham from Grosse Pointe is a pretty simple shot straight north, especially if you connect to Woodward. Traffic was light and there was enough time for me to think about what I'd learned so far.

I've never been a big believer in instinct as I usually ignore the little whispers my subconscious gives me. But I had a definite feeling something was a little bit off. I couldn't tell if it was the case, that maybe it was heading in a different direction than I had intended, or if it was something else entirely.

In any event, I found the address of Platinum Escorts and it threw me for a loop. It was one of the biggest buildings in the little downtown of Birmingham, and I knew it was a group of million-dollar condominiums. The place was simply called Rothwell, after the street upon which the lavishly constructed structure had been built.

The only available parking was in a public structure a block away so I left the car there and walked back over to Rothwell where a doorman let me in.

The lobby was spacious with a black marble floor, a few plants, and fresh flowers in funky pottery vases. A bank of elevators sat off to my left. There was a concierge or finely dressed security guard sitting behind a desk on the right.

Now I had a dilemma.

How the hell was I going to ask for Platinum Escorts? There was no way they went by that name. Argyle? Was there really a guy named Argyle? Or gal?

I crossed the lobby to the slim black desk behind which a thin man with a pencil mustache sat.

"Hi, I'm here to see the Argyles," I said. I figured since I didn't know the gender, referring to the name as a couple would hit both possibilities.

"Would you like me to ring them?" he asked, obviously wondering why I wasn't calling them myself. But I didn't have an apartment number and even if I wanted to take a chance and get on the elevator, I figured they required a key.

"Yes, please," I said.

"May I tell them who is calling?"

I took a gamble and said, "Mr. Nix."

The little, wispy guy spoke into the phone and then stood up and led me to the elevator. He had on a cologne that smelled like someone had stuck a stalk of vanilla bean into a jar of formaldehyde.

I stepped inside the elevator and he used his key and then pressed the button for the third floor. He started to step out.

"You know, I've got a bit of dyslexia," I said. "I can't remember are they in three–"

"Three twenty-five," he said. His voice was high and crisp with a tone that sounded like he wasn't buying my bullshit but didn't really care.

The elevator shut and even though I didn't feel it move, a

moment later it deposited me on the third floor. It was a dark hallway, with purple carpet and silvery walls.

I went down to three twenty-five and used the silver knocker to announce my presence. The door opened and I saw a woman with thick black glasses and a short, black bob haircut.

"Oh!" she said.

"Hi, Nix sent me," I said simply. The only way to play this one out was to go with the flow.

She didn't bat an eye. "Jordy!" she called out.

From a room off of the main living area a young man emerged. He had on jeans, was barefoot, and a black T-shirt with holes in it.

"Who are you?" he asked.

Jesus, the kid couldn't have been more than eighteen years old. In fact, if I had to guess I would say he was still in high school. Maybe a junior or something.

Taking a closer look, though, I saw the resemblance to the woman.

"Um, can we talk privately?" I asked.

"Is everything okay, Jordy?" the woman asked. She had seemed totally casual before but now seeing her son's reaction she sensed something might be wrong. A mother's instinct and all that.

"Yeah, Mom, it's fine," he said, looking at me a bit dismissively. As in, *what the hell could this guy possibly do to me?*

She turned and now reassured, smiled at me. "Can I get you anything to drink?"

"Let's go," Jordy said before I could answer and I followed him into the next room where he shut the door behind us.

It was set up like an office even though I suspected it was

a spare bedroom. There was a desk, with two computer screens, a black leather couch and a television with a gaming console.

"This is Platinum Escorts?" I asked. I figured there was no other way to put it.

"Yep, this is it," Jordy said.

I shook my head. "You've got to be kidding me."

He looked at me with mild curiosity. "Did Nix really send you?"

I shook my head.

"Then who the hell are you?"

"A potential customer. With a lot of money to spend," I said. "But first I want to know more about your operation before I invest."

"It's not what you think," he said. "It's really just an exchange server, like a virtual check out register. And I just take a small percentage off the top." He narrowed his eyes at me. "I think you're full of shit, by the way. And I know you're not a cop. Who are you and why did you say Nix sent you?"

"I don't know," I admitted. "I mean, I don't know why I said that. I'm a private investigator looking into the disappearance of Kierra Cotton. You probably knew her as Jade."

The kid pulled out a can of Red Bull and took a drink. "Huh, I didn't know she was missing."

"Do you know anything about where she went?" I asked.

"I just said I didn't know she was missing," he said, like he was talking to someone with learning disabilities.

"But can you look at her...transactions?" I ventured.

"No, listen, you don't know how this works. I'm basically running an encrypted server. The reason the cops don't bother me, and the reason I am talking to you so freely is that I'm not really doing anything illegal," he said. This kid was smart. I wondered if he would ever put his intellect to use for something other than exploiting young women for money. "There are other parts of this that are highly illegal, but I'm not involved in those."

"I see," I said, even though I really didn't.

"I only know Jade from her name and the images on the site, which I check out occasionally," he said, and he sneaked a glance over my shoulder to make sure his Mom wasn't listening.

But I was eighteen once and I figured he might have gotten to know some of the girls on a personal level, if he had the chance.

"So you can't tell me anything about who she might have been seeing? Who her clients were?"

He shook his head. "Think of it like a department store. You know how they hire people to make up those fancy displays in the front of the store? The window displays?"

"Yeah."

"That's all I do, really. I don't know anything else," he said. "From what I hear, though, asking a lot of questions about the other stuff is dangerous business. That's why I don't do it. You kind of look like a dumbass, though."

Now it was my turn to laugh. "Thank you for that keen observation," I said. But I knew this was going nowhere.

I stood up and was about to say goodbye.

"I kind of figured you would be into T-girls," he said knowingly and then laughed.

"Tea girls? What's a tea girl?" I said.

He laughed again, even harder.

"What?" I said. "Is that like slang for an Asian? Like a Geisha girl? A tea girl?"

He laughed again, drained the rest of his Red Bull.

"Get the fuck outta here," he said.

32

I f there was one thing Clay could say about this snotty little town they called Birmingham, it would have to be that it represented everything he hated about people. A bunch of flaming idiots disguised as men wearing bright colored shirts and walking around in sandals. He wanted to beat the shit out of everyone he saw, women and children included.

But he couldn't.

Being in stakeout mode wasn't easy in this place. He realized he stuck out like a whore in the church choir.

The big old truck, his tattoos. Not the kind of thing you saw in this dumb ass place.

But this is where the Rockne guy, the private investigator, decided to drive so he, Clay, had to follow. Clay had no idea why the dude was coming to Birmingham.

The girl, Jade, was a fucking hooker. Unless she turned tricks here or something. Some of these old, rich guys probably hired chicks all the time. Only way they could get pussy, probably. They had to pay for it and they probably paid top dollar. Of course, as the old saying went, one way or another you *always* ended up paying for it.

Clay wondered if maybe that's what the PI was doing here. Tracking down Jade's clients. That made sense. But how would you figure out who she was screwing? Not like these girls kept a written record of their meetings. Not the smart ones, anyway. If there was such a thing as a smart hooker. He thought there probably wasn't.

Maybe the PI was using Jade's phone. But if she was missing, chances were, her phone was gone, too.

He had parked in front of a little church just down from the fancy building Rockne had gone into. Now, he considered moving. Clay hadn't seen any cops yet, but it was better to be moving than to sit still too long in a place like this.

He was reaching for the key to fire the truck back up when Rockne walked out of the building.

Huh, he thought. That hadn't taken long.

Probably a dead end.

Clay watched as Rockne walked back to the parking garage, then waited until he came out. He started the truck up but stayed well behind Rockne. The truck wasn't the best choice to follow someone and he had gotten too close a couple of times to Rockne on the freeway.

He decided to take a chance that the PI would go back to Grosse Pointe and probably follow the same route, so he pulled out ahead of his target on Woodward, and followed it toward the freeway.

Sure enough, he saw Rockne behind him. That was the best way to tail someone, Clay reminded himself. Get in front of them so they think there's no possible reason to be suspicious.

Sure enough, Rockne went all the way back to Grosse Pointe, and Clay turned off before he did, then went the other way on a surface street until he was out of sight, then he doubled back.

Clay spotted Rockne getting off the same freeway exit he'd used to start the trip, and he followed him into a little residential area a few blocks off of Mack Avenue until he pulled up into a driveway.

The house was a two-story brick home and there was a woman in front with a garden hose watering some plants.

Well isn't that just all cute and charming, Clay thought.

He had to turn off before he got to the block and then he looped around until he was facing it from the other direction.

Even though he was a half a block away, Clay liked what he saw with the woman. She had long, dark hair and was wearing a pair of shorts with a T-shirt. The shorts showed off some nice legs, a pretty good ass, and her boobs looked nice. Big enough to see from here, they were probably even larger up close. Larger and succulent, he thought. *Or should he say...suckulent*. Haha.

It looked like there was a rugrat running around because when Rockne got out of his car, it came running up to him.

Clay took out the sheet of paper and jotted down the street names of the intersection so he would remember. He decided he'd learned enough about Rockne. He needed to go check out the asshole's office now.

John Wayne had written that down for him, too.

He put the truck in gear but he couldn't stop thinking about that woman with the garden hose.

Oh, I'll give you a hose you can hold onto, he thought.

Clay laughed as he drove away.

33

Being a private investigator requires the ability to have difficult conversations.

One day you might have to tell a woman that her suspicions were right and her husband is doing Zumba with his personal trainer but neither of them wear clothes when they do it.

Or maybe it's telling an old man that his punk kid had emptied the bank account and run off to Alaska to eat blubber with his escaped convict girlfriend.

That last one hadn't happened but it sounded like a fun case.

But the conversation I was about to have with Marvin and Arnella Cotton was not going to be easy.

I had made a call to them saying I had some follow-up questions regarding the case, and they invited me over to their house. At least that part was good. Asking the kind of questions I had to ask would be better for them in the comfort of their own home.

At least that's what I told myself as I pulled up to their extremely modest single story home within a stone's throw of Mack Avenue. They lived two doors down from the dry cleaner where Anna took my shirts every few weeks.

Marvin answered the door and invited me into the living room, where Arnella was already sitting.

"Want something to drink?" he asked. I could tell he was uncomfortable, sheepish almost. And I could also tell that Arnella looked angry. She sat with her legs crossed in a wingback chair, and her foot was tapping the air not so much in rhythm, but like she was itching to kick someone's ass.

That particular ass could in theory belong to a wonderful local private investigator who was just trying to do the right thing.

I would be less of a man if I didn't admit that I hoped she was thinking of kicking her husband's ass and not yours truly.

"No thanks," I said.

Marvin sat on the couch, and I sat in a matching wingback chair. It was a little sitting area facing a fireplace that looked like it had never been used. There was a vase on the fireplace mantle and a picture of Kierra. It looked like her graduation picture from high school. She didn't look anything like that now, I thought.

"So is there news?" Marvin asked, getting right to the point.

"Yes and no," I said. I then explained that I had been able to track some of Kierra's movements but that there was still no clear indication of where she was or what had happened to her.

"Are you sure she was in Traverse City?" Arnella asked me. Her voice was full of skepticism.

I pulled out my phone and showed her the photo. "This was taken by a photographer who covered the convention."

"I see," Arnella said. She shot a glance over at Marvin that seemed full of hostility. "I'm sure she was someone's guest there."

She placed a fair amount of emphasis on the word guest, and it wasn't a good kind of emphasis.

"I don't have any clear indication of how she got there or who she was with," I answered, telling the truth.

"What about AJ?" Marvin asked.

I shook my head. "I haven't been able to find him. I stopped by his house and no one has seen him for the past few days."

"Maybe he's with Kierra," Marvin said.

"Maybe," I said in as neutral a tone as possible.

"What else?" Arnella asked.

I hesitated, even though I had gone over all of the possible ways of bringing the issue up. In the end, I tried to be as direct as possible.

"Is Kierra transsexual?" The word hung in the room and no one moved.

"Damn you," Arnella said to Marvin. She got up and left the room.

Marvin looked at me. "I need a drink. Care to join me?"

"Okay."

He left, and returned with two glasses of whiskey.

"You should have told me, Marvin."

"I know," he said, sitting on the couch with a tired resignation. "I just hoped that her gender issue wasn't a factor. But I should have known it would come up."

"Technically, it hasn't come up as having to do with anything," I said. "But obviously it raises some questions."

He nodded. "Yes, she wanted to get the operation to transition, but we don't have that kind of money. And it's not covered by insurance."

That information fell into place. No wonder she was working as an escort. It was a way to raise cash. Maybe a lot of cash. And maybe real fast.

I took a drink of the whiskey and Marvin seemed to gulp at his.

"That's why Arnella didn't want me to hire you," he admitted. I had already figured that but I didn't stop him. "And why she tried to get you to drop the case. She figures the less people who know, the better."

"Well, I'm not planning on telling anyone," I pointed out.

"I appreciate it. About that, I'm about at my limit in terms of how much more I can pay you," he said.

"Bullshit," a voice said behind me. Arnella was standing in the space between the living room and the kitchen.

"You've come this far, now you know why she was doing what she was doing," Arnella said. "Finish it. Find her, Mr. Rockne. Before something bad happens to her, if it already hasn't."

She glared at both me and Marvin, then left. I heard the back door to the house slam shut.

Marvin and I sat there a little longer. His whiskey glass was empty but he seemed to have no interest in remedying that situation. I sipped at mine some more. Marvin glanced up at the photo of Kierra on the mantle a couple of times.

"What do you think, John?" he said, his voice so soft I could barely hear it. "Where do you think she is?"

With everything in my heart I wanted to give him an answer.

But I didn't have one to give.

34

The Cadieux Café doesn't sound like a cop bar, but it's technically in Detroit, and that's where I agreed to meet the cop son of Nate's colleague.

It was right on Cadieux, not surprisingly, just down from the border with Grosse Pointe and it was known for its feather bowling courts.

If you've never been to Michigan or to Belgium, it's a strange sport to describe. Basically, you stick a feather in the ground and then roll these things that look like wooden cheese wheels and you try to get them as close to the feather as you can. Kind of like horseshoes.

I feather bowled once but I was quite drunk at the time, so it just may have been a bad dream.

The cop was sitting at the bar, chatting up a bartender with a tight T-shirt and skinny jeans who was old enough to be his mother. Neither one seemed to notice her age, though.

"Are you Jeff?" I asked the young man. He turned initially and gave me that cop look, but seeing that I wasn't trying to horn in on his action, he mellowed right away.

"I'm John Rockne, your Dad works with my friend Nate," I said. Looking at the bartender I said, "put his beer on my tab and we'll each take another."

She went about her business and I sat on the bar stool next to him.

"Thanks," he said, tipping his beer toward me and he polished it off with a couple long pulls.

Jeff was a young guy, way too young to me. Another sign I was getting old. He was probably in his late twenties but it looked like he should be graduating from high school. He was blonde with a goatee and his arms were thick with muscles, bulging out from beneath the dark blue shirt.

"I'm off duty," he said. "I usually stop by here after work to cool off."

"Me too," I replied. Our beers came and I took a drink, not realizing how thirsty I was and how good a cold beer would taste right about now.

"So I wanted to ask you about the night of the big party at the mayor's mansion. Nate said you were on duty and got called to that one."

He laughed. "Yeah, what the hell was that all about? I mean, you're the frickin' mayor and you can't control your own party? And you're supposed to be in charge of an entire city?"

He laughed, revealing some pretty crooked teeth. I wondered when the police force's dental plan kicked in.

"So it got pretty out of control?" I asked.

"Not as bad as the papers made it sound, honestly," he said. "We had a few drunk and disorderlies, a couple of assaults, open intoxicants, minor possessions. Really the crime was that the party got too big and I think, my own personal opinion, is that people figured they were above the law."

Above the law. Yeah, I could see that. Especially if the law worked for you like an arrogant mayor might believe.

"Easy to do when you're partying with the mayor," I pointed out.

"Right," Jeff said. "I mean, that's why people were out in the street and how it got too rowdy."

"Did you arrest anyone?" I asked.

"No, I let everyone off with a warning, as long as they weren't doing anything too crazy," he said. "Mainly because I hate paperwork. A couple of buddies of mine had to pepper spray a guy, though. He went to jail."

"Were there a lot of women at the party?"

"Tons of them, dude," he said. His eyes kind of lit up. He was a young man, after all. "A ton of hotties. I think some of them were working the party, if you know what I mean."

I pulled out my phone and showed him the picture of Kierra at the auto convention.

"Do you think you saw her there?" I asked.

He took the phone and using his fingers enlarged it so he could see her face better.

"No, I don't think so," he answered. But he was clearly uncertain. "She looks kind of young. And she's pretty beautiful. I think I would have remembered her if I'd seen her."

"Do you guys know a man named Nix? Works security sometimes for the mayor?"

"Doesn't ring a bell," Jeff said. "But those guys the mayor's got working for him? I'd be surprised if they go by their real names. Some real shady characters, is what I hear."

I put my phone on the bar and tried to figure out what to do next. It still seemed like a good bet that the second of Kierra's big scores was the mayor's party, mainly because I had seen or read nothing else that might qualify. Unless it was a private "date" with a wealthy benefactor.

That thought depressed me.

There would be no way for me to track that down. Considering that Platinum Escorts was a dead-end even the police didn't bother with.

"Everyone says Mayor Mahorn is all about pay to play, and from what I hear there's a lot of paying and a lot playing," Jeff said.

"That's why they call him Horny Mahorn, right?" I asked.

The young cop laughed. "Yep, I heard that one, too."

He took a drink of his beer, grabbed my phone and looked at the picture of Kierra again.

"Looks like Vaughn had his eye on this girl, huh?"

I put my beer down.

"Who?"

"Vaughn," he said as he put my phone down and pointed at the picture.

He must have seen the look of confusion on my face.

With his finger he tapped directly on the back of the silver-haired man's head.

"Michael Vaughn," he said. "I'd recognize that hair anywhere. He's a big lawyer. Does a ton of work for the mayor. And his wife's a judge."

Jeff smirked.

"Don't think she'd be too crazy about that picture, though," he added.

35

"I fucking knew it!" Nate exclaimed over the phone. "I knew it was him, I just couldn't place it."

"Okay, get over yourself," I said. "So tell me about him."

"He's connected up the wazoo to anyone who's anyone in Detroit," Nate said, all excited. He lived for this kind of thing. He smelled a good story, and so did I. I wasn't interested in it for that, though. I felt like I was finally closing in on what might have happened to Kierra.

"He's *totally* in tight with Mahorn," Nate continued. "He's also got connections with the Irish mob and his wife's a freaking judge. How great is that for a lawyer?"

That did present a lot of interesting angles. I wondered how much of Vaughn's influence was dependent upon his ability to get favors in court.

"So does he argue his cases to her?" I asked. "Isn't that a conflict of interest? Wouldn't she have to recuse herself from any of his cases?"

"Of course he doesn't directly argue his cases, that would

be a total conflict of interest. Anything they did that way
would get tossed out."

"So what do they do?"

"Well, there are all kinds of rumors."

"Like what?"

"Just that clients of Vaughn's firm have a very good
track record of winning cases," Nate said. "He's obviously
not the only lawyer at the firm. They've got dozens
of them."

"So the rumor is she gives out preferential judgments if
the case is handled by her husband's firm."

"Sure," Nate said.

"It probably helps his business," I said. "Hire the lawyer
whose wife is a judge."

"I'm sure Mahorn is well aware of it, as are his other big
political clients," Nate said. "Man, John, if he's involved in
this girl's disappearance you'd better really watch your back.
This ain't the minor leagues. You're playing with the big
boys now."

"Thanks for that tip, Nate," I said.

He couldn't tell me anything else so we disconnected
and I immediately went to my office and logged onto the
local news websites, searching for any news stories and
photographs of Michael Vaughn and his wife.

I found out quickly that his wife's name was Claire
Vaughn. I saw pictures of them together at political
fundraisers. At art gallery openings. With local celebrities.
They were clearly what you would call a power couple.

A recent story had made the rounds about the judge
giving a very light sentence to a felon with a long criminal
history, a scary-looking white guy named Clay Hitchfield.
There was a picture of him and for some reason he looked
familiar. But I was sure I'd never met him. I stared at his

picture a little longer. Something about it made me uneasy but I couldn't figure out what.

I continued reading articles about the Vaughns and saw that they also happened to live in Grosse Pointe. One of the news stories was about their home. A famous structure built in the early part of the century by a wealthy Grosse Pointe family. The Vaughns had renovated it, of course, and it was one of the finest private homes in Grosse Pointe, which was saying something.

I thought, *what the hell.* They probably wouldn't be home, but I knew exactly where that house was.

As quickly as I could I closed up the office and drove out of the Village, then through a section of Grosse Pointe known as The Hill, until I got to a street called Heartmoor. There were only a few homes on the block because each house was enormous. These were estates and certainly worth millions upon millions of dollars. But what's that to a successful partner in a big law firm and a judge?

Talk about your dual income.

Without a moment's hesitation I pulled right into the big driveway, thankful there was no gate.

I parked, and walked up to the massive set of front doors. I rang the bell and waited.

A young woman opened the door.

"Hello, my name is John Rockne and I would love to talk to Michael Vaughn, Claire Vaughn, or both of them if they're available."

She gave me an odd look then said, "Wait just a minute, please."

She shut the door and I was sure it automatically locked.

A full five minutes passed before the man in the photo opened the door. He was huge. At least 6'5" with broad shoulders and a massive head of silver hair.

Put a cowboy hat on his head and the bastard looked like John Wayne.

He stared at me and I could see an almost bemused expression on his face. But there was something else.

I decided it was fatigue.

Michael Vaughn looked very, very tired.

"What can I do for you?" he said.

"Answer some questions about the disappearance of Kierra Cotton," I answered.

There was no way in hell he was going to let me into the house. I knew it with every fiber of my being. All of my years as a private investigator helped me to prepare for either a punch or an outright attack. He was going to tell me to get my ass off his property. I knew it. One hundred percent sure.

And then he almost smiled.

"Come in, Mr. Rockne," he said. His voice was deep and powerful. Not a man to be trifled with.

He walked me through the palatial foyer into a sitting room that looked casual but was adorned with several oil paintings that were clearly old and expensive. I recognized the woman sitting on the white couch to be Claire Vaughn.

"Hello," I said, not sure if I should call her the Judge, Mrs. Vaughn, or Your Honor. So I just skipped it.

Michael Vaughn sat next to her and he gestured toward a chair across from them. I sat, and realized I was about to address a high-powered attorney and a judge all at once.

"I'm investigating the disappearance of a young woman named Kierra Cotton," I said.

"What does that have to do with us?" the woman snapped. Her face was rigid and she had red hair piled high on her head. And she had crazy eyes. I would not want to be seated across from her in a court.

On the contrary, Michael Vaughn looked totally relaxed.

It occurred to me that not only would I have to be really careful with what I said, but that it probably didn't matter because if they wanted to they could probably get me locked up and then hauled in front of her.

"Mr. Vaughn, does the name ring a bell?"

"No," he said. But he had a twinkle in his eye.

Why was he enjoying this? I wondered.

"I'd like to show you a photo if I could," I began.

"Mr. Rockne, you are on dangerous ground here," Judge Vaughn said, in a voice that I was sure she used to intimidate lawyers and their clients. "If you so much as breathe a word that would constitute defamation of character or slander, we will sue you and you will lose everything you have."

The ferocity of her words took me back, but only slightly.

"So do you want to see the photograph or not?"

"I want to know exactly why you're here," Michael Vaughn interjected. "Why you think this girl's disappearance has anything to do with me?" he said.

I understood that's why he let me inside. He only wanted to know what I knew. That was fine with me.

So I used my words carefully, but I really figured it wouldn't matter. But I did know enough about the law to use certain words.

"There is a possibility that you were at the same auto convention as Kierra, and then also at the same party at the mayor's mansion as Kierra," I said. "Since those were the last two places she was seen before her disappearance, and I have a photograph that clearly shows you standing very close to her, I thought you might be able to provide some additional information."

"Julie!" Claire Vaughn called out abruptly, getting to her

feet. The young woman who answered the door appeared immediately in the doorway, her face obviously frightened.

"See this man out, now," the Judge said.

We sat there in silence. I looked at Michael Vaughn and he seemed to be looking over the top of my head to somewhere in the distance.

Julie, the woman who had let me in, hurried into the room. She looked at me, panic on her face.

I got to my feet and nobody said a word. I took out my business card and placed it on a table that held a Tiffany lamp. Original, I was sure.

"Here's my card if you think of anything."

Nobody answered as I was escorted out of the house.

36

"Yo, Chief," I said, dropping into a chair across from the Chief of Police in Grosse Pointe.

My sister Ellen looked at me.

"Sorry, I'm not looking to hire a personal assistant," she said. "Besides, I don't think you're qualified."

This is how things work in the Rockne family.

"My hazmat suit is at the cleaners anyway," I said. "So I wouldn't be available to start."

She sighed and looked over my shoulder as a couple of Grosse Pointe cops walked by.

"What can I do for you, sir?" she said, her snark in full effect.

I filled her in regarding what I'd learned about Kierra Cotton and my meeting with the Vaughns.

"I've heard of them," she said. "Or I should say her. A few cops have gone up before her. They say she's tough but unpredictable."

"I'm surprised you two aren't friends," I pointed out.

"Seriously, do you need something?" she said. "I've got

work to do and the taxpayers are always watching. If you paid taxes, you would know what I mean."

"Clay Hitchfield," I said.

"Who?"

"Clay Hitchfield. He was one of Judge Vaughn's cases and he got off with a fairly light sentence."

"So?"

"Well, I had to run up to Birmingham to interview a possible lead in the case and I had this weird feeling I was being followed," I said. "And then when I read about this guy, I got to thinking that maybe I had seen him on that trip. Like maybe he'd been following me. And if so, I was wondering if he had anything to do with my case."

Ellen sighed again and leaned forward and tapped on her computer.

She waited a bit and then nodded.

"Yeah, he's not exactly an upstanding citizen," she said. "Multiple arrests that go way back. Grand theft. Assault. Burglary. More assaults. Possession."

I watched her scroll down the list and then her brow furrowed.

"Does seem like he got off pretty easy for the last thing," she said. "Aggravated assault."

"Any address for him?"

She shook her head. "You could try his parole officer but I doubt they'd give it up to a private investigator, or whatever it is you're calling yourself these days."

This was true. The part about parole officers not giving out addresses like candy. I had a few ways to get that kind of information, though.

While I was pleased I had connected a couple more dots, now I was really afraid for Kierra. If the Vaughns had decided to get rid of her, they had the perfect guy for the job.

I got to my feet. "Thank you for your help, Chief. I'll be sure to let the city know they're in good hands."

"If you're messing around with Clay Hitchfield I hope you're being careful," she said. "I'd say that I hope you're being smart but we both know that's not an option for you."

Letting Ellen get the last word was my idea of charity. My good deed for the day. Because amongst the smart aleck stuff, I could have sworn that she told me to be careful. I was downright touched.

Almost.

37

In the parking lot outside the police station, I got behind the wheel of the minivan but didn't turn the ignition.

Various scenarios were going through my mind.

What was Michael Vaughn doing with Kierra? Had he set something up with her for Mayor Horny Mahorny? Was she one of the mayor's girls and Vaughn was basically a pimp? But if she had a pimp, then why did she need an escort service?

It didn't make sense.

And would the husband of a judge really be working on the side as a pimp? That was ridiculous. The Vaughn estate was worth millions and it was highly unlikely they needed any extra money.

Nix.

What about Nix?

He, too, had most likely been at both events. But he hadn't been pictured with Kierra. Was Nix a pimp? Was he the one who had arranged for Kierra to be at the auto convention and the mayor's party?

Was Vaughn one of Nix's clients? And Nix was the one running Kierra? Did Kierra's gender have anything to do with her disappearance?

It felt like there was something else I was missing. Something that brushed up against a couple of other ideas but that resisted being formed into a complete thought. It was frustrating.

I turned the key and started the engine, put the van in gear and pulled back out onto Jefferson. Home was only about a forty-second drive from the police station and when I was halfway there my phone rang.

The caller ID told me it was Lace.

Now that was a surprise.

"Hello?" I said.

"John?" she asked. I had a strange moment of hesitation where I was wondering if she got me confused with one of her johns, as opposed to actually remembering my first name.

"Lace?" I answered.

This time, she hesitated. "This is Rockne, the private investigator, right?" she said. She sounded sober, which was good. And her voice was totally different. Not the breathless words of someone stoned out of their mind.

"Yeah, what's up?" I asked.

I turned onto my street.

"Um, well I think I just got a message from Jade," she said. "You know, Kierra."

Holy shit.

I pulled into the driveway, parked and shut off the car.

"What did the message say?"

"That she was fine. And not to worry."

Could I believe her? She seemed sober and in her own garbled way, she had tried to tell me about Grandmaster D.

"Was it a voice message?" I asked. "Or a text?"

"It was a text," she said. "That's why I'm not so sure."

Hmm. I thought about that. Hope flared up as I asked the next question.

"So you have the number, then, right?"

"Yeah, that's what's kind of weird, too," she said.

I had gotten out of the car and was about to unlock the back door to the house. I was already thinking of the notepad and pen Anna always kept in the little drawer by the part of the kitchen countertop we used as a desk.

"What?" I said.

"It's a California area code," she said.

California? Was she there? Or was she using a cell phone belonging to someone from out there?

"Okay, why don't you forward the message to me and I'll check it out," I said.

I opened the door and stepped inside.

Lace ended the call so she could send me the text and I called out to see if Anna was home or if she was still at school picking up the kids.

The message from Lace popped onto my phone and I saw the number for myself.

"California," I said. "Who would have thought–"

A shock of pain erupted at the back of my neck and a bright flash of light exploded across my vision. I took a step forward and then felt myself falling. There was a loud noise and the last thing I remembered was the idea that it was probably the sound of my head hitting the floor.

38

I smelled coffee.

Felt water on my face and opened my eyes.

Clay Hitchfield stood before me, our glass coffee pot in his hand. I realized it wasn't water on my face, but leftover coffee that he'd poured on me.

"They say coffee helps you wake up," Hitchfield said and he laughed. His teeth were horrible and crooked, his skinny arms covered with tattoos and in his other hand was a gun.

He swung the coffee pot and hit me on the side of the face.

It hurt a little, but I still felt kind of numb and my neck wouldn't move.

I knew this, because I wanted to see the kitchen clock, above the sink.

How long had I been out?

Whatever was causing my neck to freeze suddenly unstuck and I caught a quick glimpse of the clock. Anna would be getting home any minute, unless she had stopped to chat with the other Moms. Sometimes she did that. I prayed that's what she was doing now.

I struggled to move, but realized my hands were taped, too.

He threw the coffee pot across the kitchen and it landed in the sink where it shattered.

I had to get this bastard out of here.

With his other hand, he grabbed my cell phone off the kitchen counter.

"What's this message mean?" he said. "I'm fine. Don't worry. And then a phone number."

He used a singsongy voice to imitate the message. Like it was a bratty teenager who had left the text.

"It's from Jade, she's back in town," I said. "I'm supposed to meet her but if I'm not there in ten minutes, she's going to disappear again."

He squinted his beady little eyes at me.

"You can't bullshit me," he said. "Others have tried. All have failed."

He walked over and opened the door to the fridge, pulled out a plastic dish full of chicken tenders and started eating them. Hitchfield tore at the chicken with an animal savagery.

"Fuck I'm hungry. I love chicken nuggets," he said. "Your nice lookin' bitch make these? Where the hell is she at?" he said. He licked his lips.

"She's at her parents with the kids, they're having dinner there and sleeping over."

He laughed. "I think you're full of shit. I liked the look of her and I haven't had a clean woman in awhile."

Hitchfield looked at my phone, still in his hand.

"So where are you supposedly meeting her?" he asked. He threw the rest of the chicken across kitchen into the sink.

I thought as fast as I could seeing how my skull felt like it was wrapped too tight around my brain. Like it was going to explode. A sharp pain kept pulsating between my eyes. It made me squint.

"I'm supposed to go to a bar where she's going to call me and where she can watch me," I said. I tried to make my voice sound as assured as possible. "If there aren't any cops around then she's going to talk to me. But I have to be there in less than five minutes. "

Hitchfield used his fingers to pick pieces of chicken from between his teeth. He licked his lips again and looked around the kitchen. His beady eyes bore down on me and he smiled. With those messed up chompers, though, it looked more like a ghastly grimace.

He made his decision and put my phone into his pocket, grabbed my arm and hoisted me to my feet.

"If you're lying, I'm going to blow your brains out," he said. "And then I'm going to come right back here and fuck your wife's brains out."

39

It was hard to believe in broad daylight I was being led out to the sidewalk and marched down the street with my hands bound.

But Hitchfield had put a kitchen towel over my hands to hide the tape. I knew it looked strange but I had my doubts if it looked weird enough for someone to call the cops. Hitchfield was a weird-looking guy, though. I wondered if my nosy neighbor Mrs. Ratcliffe might be watching out her window. Maybe she'd turn off Wheel of Fortune or whatever the hell she watched all day and call the damn cops. Call my sister, Ellen.

Even as I imagined the scenario I knew it wouldn't happen.

Hitchfield prodded me forward and when we crossed the next street I saw his vehicle. And as soon as the big Ram truck came into view, I knew where I'd seen him. In Birmingham. I'd spotted that truck twice and must have seen his face. And then I had a quick flashback to when I'd staked out the trap house looking for AJ.

Oh my God, AJ.

I suddenly realized why no one had heard from him in a few days.

Goddamnit. I should have listened to my instincts.

I thought of all the times I complained about how everyone in Grosse Pointe loved to get into everyone else's business, but right now, I wished to God someone would see that I was walking awkwardly down the street with a guy who looked like he just walked out of prison.

Nope, it wasn't gonna happen.

But God help it if I put the yard waste out a day early and Anna's phone would be ringing off the hook by crotchety old folks saying they'd call the city if I didn't bring the garbage cans back. Code violation!

Hitchfield walked me to the passenger side of the big truck, opened the door and pushed me inside.

"Make a move and I'll shoot you right now," he said.

He walked around the front of the truck, keeping his eyes on me the whole time and then got behind the wheel. He slammed his door shut and locked both of our doors.

"Where we going?" he said. "And let me remind you. If this is all bullshit I'm going to put a bullet in your brain and come right back to your house and head straight into your wife's britches.

Britches?

"Cadieux Café," I said, a plan coming together in my mind. Not much of one. But it was all I could muster. "Turn right up here, then left on Cadieux. It's only about six blocks away."

"Thought you said you were meeting her at a bar." His beady eyes focused on me. It was his attempt at intimidation. I didn't have the heart to tell him that it wasn't working because I was beyond that point.

"It is a bar," I said.

"But it's called a café?" he asked as he put the big truck into gear. "That doesn't make a fucking lick of sense. People go in think they can get some French Toast or something? I hate uppity people. Always putting on airs."

I didn't quite know what to say to that so I stayed silent.

"How come you don't carry a gun?" he asked me. "I looked after I decked you. And you call yourself a private eye? What a joke. Coming after people like me without a weapon? That's just suicide, you stupid ass."

"Usually I don't need one," I said.

"Yeah, right," he said. "You don't need one because you wouldn't use it anyway. Too afraid. You're just a pussy pretending to be some kind of neighborhood cop. I hate people like you."

"That's too bad because I'm quite fond of you," I said.

He pulled into the Cadieux Café's parking lot and I prayed to God that my feeble plan would work out. That Jeff, the young cop who'd told me about the mayor's party was at the bar like he'd told me he usually does after work. It was a stretch, but it was the only thing I could think of.

"She calling you on a pay phone or what?"

I laughed. "A pay phone? What the hell? You stuck in 1980? There aren't pay phones anymore."

He reached over and half-punched me in the face but I managed to twist my head so it was more of a glancing blow.

"Keep it up, smart-ass," he said. "Your wife is already going to be screaming for mercy. Maybe I'll go even harder on her than I had planned."

I'd tried hard to keep my anger in check, but I swore if he said one more thing about Anna I was going to take that gun away from him and shove it up his ass.

"Jade said she's going to call the bar and ask the bartender if I'm there," I explained patiently but through my gritted teeth. "That's the plan. Do you get it?" My tone was completely patronizing but it seemed to go right over his shaved head.

"Okay, let's go," he said.

He dragged me out, put the kitchen towel back over my hands and we walked inside.

I saw right away that my plan had failed miserably.

Not only was Jeff not there, there wasn't a single person at the bar. The place was completely empty.

Shit.

Now what was I going to do?

Hitchfield pushed me forward and had me sit on the stool at the far left, up against the wall, so he could pin me in.

He'd put his gun in his waistband and pulled his shirt over it.

The bartender appeared from out of a room behind the bar and walked over. She was the same middle-aged woman with the impressive attributes who had served me when I came to talk to Jeff. Different T-shirt, but it was another tight one.

"Two beers," Hitchfield said.

I felt the muzzle of his gun press into my side.

"All right," she said.

She brought the beers and Hitchfield threw a ten dollar bill on the bar. When she brought the change back, he scooped it all up except for fifty cents.

Jeez, a bad tipper, too.

I had no way of drinking the beer, but Hitchfield took a long pull of his and glanced at the clock over the bar. When the bartender slipped into the back room, probably for a smoke, he leaned forward and whispered in my ear.

"I'm giving you five minutes or until I finish these beers," he said. "Whichever comes first."

With that, he drained the rest of his first beer in three giant gulps. Then he winked at me.

He glanced toward the back room to make sure the bartender wasn't watching then slid my beer in front of him and put his empty in front of me.

We waited in silence, except for the jukebox playing in the background. Some country song about someone buying a boat.

A boat sounded like a nice place to be, I thought.

Anywhere seemed like a better place to be than right here. Right now.

The bartender came back over, saw my empty and asked me if I wanted a refill.

Hitchfield's gun went into my ribs again.

"No thanks," I said.

She left and it took him another five minutes to finish the second beer.

By then, we'd been there at least ten minutes and I desperately tried to think of something to keep him there, but I drew a blank.

I tried to catch the bartender's eye and thought about asking if Jeff was coming in but I figured that wouldn't accomplish much.

Hitchfield slammed down his second beer bottle, now empty, onto the bar.

"Let's go," he said softly.

The bartender reappeared upon hearing the sound of the empty bottle, but Hitchfield gave her a little wave. She collected the empties and Hitchfield got to his feet. He hesitated until the bartender's back was turned then he hoisted me up.

We walked to the front door, me leading the way so Hitchfield could block the view of the bartender and we made it outside.

"Can't wait to have some quality time with your wife, John" Hitchfield said. He gave a little giggle and he seemed extremely happy that Jade hadn't appeared. It was all the excuse he was going to need.

He opened the passenger door and pushed me in none too gently. I waited for the door to slam shut but it didn't.

Instead, I heard the sound of tires on gravel.

I turned and looked.

Nix stood there, looking at me.

Behind him, I saw two big guys in black suits shoving Hitchfield into the back seat of their big black SUV.

Nix pulled out a switchblade and I held my hands out.

I had no idea if he was going to stab me or free me.

Without taking his eyes from my face, he sliced through the duct tape.

"There's a small price for the service I just provided," he said.

"Name it," I said. My wrists were rubbed raw.

"All I want is a little gap in your memory that includes seeing me and my guys here," Nix said. His eyes were flat and his voice was soft. Everything else about him had the edge I remembered.

Nix was someone I never wanted to see again.

"As far as you can remember you came here for a drink and left. Never saw anyone. Certainly not any individuals who resemble me in any way. Understand?"

"Absolutely," I said.

Nix scanned my eyes and seemed satisfied. He walked around to the passenger side of the big SUV and got inside. They drove off.

I got out of Hitchfield's truck and shut the door.
It would be a short walk home.

The flight to Los Angeles landed on time but then I had to wait in a long line for my rental car.

Traveling was not one of my favorite things to do. It always seemed like if you ever actually got a break like a flight arriving ten minutes early you then lost that ten plus another twenty waiting for the guys at the gate to get the boarding door open.

Eventually I was able to get the little envelope with my number and then I headed out to the rental car parking lot to look for my car. I found my numbered space and in it sat a little Ford Hatchback.

It was a bright blue which seemed like an odd color but I didn't care.

With a software program that provided reverse lookup for cell phone numbers I had learned that the phone used to call Lace had come from a drug rehab center just north of the city of Los Angeles.

After some consideration, I had decided it might be best for me to come out and see if that's where Kierra was before I shared the information with Marvin and Arnella.

False hope was the worst kind.

Once again using my phone's navigation I punched in the address for the facility and pulled out of the lot.

After a few twists and turns on surface streets I eventually made it to the freeway.

Traffic was light, which was a mild surprise for me because I'd heard nightmare stories about traffic jams in LA. As I drove, I thought about the case. It still wasn't exactly clear to me who had hired Hitchfield and how Kierra had managed to get out here to a drug rehab facility. The Cottons had been very clear with me that they didn't have the kind of money something like this would take.

So who was paying for it if in fact I found out that Kierra was really out here?

No answers came to me and after less than an hour on the road I pulled up into the Mountain View Center, a lodge-style main building with several smaller structures surrounding it.

I parked in a visitor spot and went inside.

"Hi, I'm here to see Kierra Cotton," I said to the perky attendant. She was a sun-kissed California girl complete with blonde hair, blue eyes and perfect teeth.

"Oh," she said with a big smile. "She's getting a lot of visitors today. Kierra is outside right now with her attorney."

Her attorney?

Why would Kierra be meeting with an attorney?

The thoughts washed over any relief I felt that I had most likely found her and that she was alive.

The front desk attendant asked for my ID and to fill out some information on a visitor's log, but the pit of my stomach had gone ice-cold. I shoved my ID at her, took the clipboard and looked around the lobby.

"That's great, do you think I could just give her a quick hello first?" I said. "Where are they meeting?"

She smiled, looked at me and then laughed. "You look harmless to me," she said. "Just promise to fill that out before you leave."

She pointed to a set of doors at the back of the room. "Those doors right there lead out to our nature preserve," she said. "That's where they are. Outside."

"Thank you," I said. I walked to the doors, opened them and stepped outside. I set the clipboard down on a bench just outside the door.

The preserve was a long sloping area of green, like a fairway on a golf course, that led down to a small pond. There was a ridge above the pond and I saw several paved pathways radiating out from the doorway in different directions.

Some of the walkways disappeared inside some impressive foliage. Giant rose bushes, and ivy-covered shrubs that had to be ten feet tall.

I scanned the area for Kierra.

Where to start?

I saw a few solitary walkers wandering around. One group of about six people appeared to be doing some kind of yoga or stretching exercise in a finely cropped circle of lawn.

And then I heard a loud crack that could only be a gunshot.

It came from the direction of the pond.

I started to run and several heads turned toward the same direction. Someone screamed and then I saw something just past the pond.

Near the edge of the tree line.

As I ran, the scene came into view. A tall man with a head of silver hair stood next to a person in a wheelchair.

Both of them were looking down at the ground.

At a third person.

I had no gun. I had no weapon at all.

But I ran as fast as I possibly could and when I came within speaking distance of them, the man turned toward me.

Michael Vaughn had a gun in his hand.

Kierra was in the wheelchair, her eyes wide with fear. She looked more like the girl in the photo on the Cotton's mantle than the skinny party girl on Instagram.

I could now see that she was tied into the wheelchair with a gag in her mouth.

The person on the ground was a woman.

With red hair.

When I was ten feet away, I stopped running and walked forward.

A pool of blood was seeping out from beneath the dead woman on the ground.

Michael Vaughn looked at me.

"Claire was going to kill her," Vaughn said.

"Why?"

He looked up at the sky.

"Was it blackmail?" I asked. That was my theory. "Was AJ blackmailing you?"

Vaughn nodded.

"I wasn't ashamed of what Kierra and I had. I was in love with her. But Claire couldn't deal with it. She didn't care about the money. She just wanted her image and prestige."

Vaughn smiled. "It wouldn't do that her husband was in love with another man."

"You sent her out here, didn't you?" I asked.

Vaughn nodded again.

"So why Hitchfield then? You knew where she was all along."

"Claire told me to. I had to play along."

"Let her go now, Michael."

"Somehow Claire figured out that I had hidden Kierra out here and she took off. That's when I called Nix."

Vaughn reached out and pulled the gag from Kierra's mouth.

"Michael, don't," she said.

"I love you," Vaughn said.

He then put the muzzle of the gun in his mouth and fired.

41

Nix disconnected from the call and slid the cell phone into his pocket.

He looked down at Clay Hitchfield.

"Before our boss left town," Nix said, "he told me he was going to put an end to this thing. And he asked me to put an end to you."

They stood in the abandoned warehouse Clay had used for his private torture sessions and body disposal.

Hitchfield was trussed up like a turkey at Thanksgiving. Nix had taken the man's gun and his knives. He'd also done a thorough inspection of the warehouse. He'd even discovered the white boy's little hidey-hole. Nix had survived this long by knowing everyone's moves well ahead of the time when he might need to take advantage of them.

So when Vaughn had called and given him his orders, he knew exactly what to do.

And where to do it.

One of Nix's men slid open the giant cement cover to the pool of acid. The other one of Nix's men dragged Hitchfield over to the opening. The white boy was terrified but trying not to act like it.

"I got money," Hitchfield said. "I can pay you more than what you're getting now. For this."

Nix smiled at him.

"You've got more money than a judge and her husband who's a partner at one of the biggest law firms in the city?" Nix said. "You know his Christmas bonus every year is probably a couple million dollars, right?

One of Nix's men laughed.

"And you're saying you've got more money than they do? And that's why you wear clothes from the dollar store and a truck from 1970?"

Hitchfield's head sagged. He looked around him. At each of Nix's men and then his gaze finally settled on Nix himself.

"I always knew some scum from the ghetto would get me in the end," he said. "Some filthy scum that never should have been born."

Nix smiled.

"Some beautiful last words right there," he said. "That's poetry, man."

He pulled the gun out of his shoulder holster and looked at it.

"I was going to be nice and shoot you first, then dump you," Nix said. He slid the gun back into its holster. "But since you're obviously an ignorant racist cracker, I'll just skip to the good part."

Nix raised his foot and kicked him in the stomach, then nodded at his men. The two of them picked up Hitchfield and tossed him into the pit of acid.

He struggled and writhed in the slime, his mouth open.

One of Nix's men used a long piece of rebar to push

Clay's head under the acid as he kicked and fought to stay above it.

After a scream or two, Clay's head went all the way under and it never came back up.

"That's the deal with racists," Nix said. "All talk, no real fight in 'em."

42

The Cottons ended up flying to Los Angeles. It took them several weeks to arrange for Kierra's release. When she was able, they all flew back to Grosse Pointe.

By then, I had already been back for awhile and was now working on several new cases.

Marvin Cotton appeared in my doorway one morning with a couple cups of coffee from the Starbucks down the street. He also had a couple pieces of lemon cake.

"Cheers," he said and we each drank our coffee. I devoured my piece of lemon cake with gusto.

"Since it's lemon, does that count as a fruit?" I asked.

"I don't see why not," Marvin answered.

Once the cake was gone I asked, "So how is she doing?"

"It's going to take some adjusting," he said. "And we were worried that when she came home she might fall back in with some of her friends. But AJ is gone and we all did some group therapy out there in Los Angeles."

"You have to," I said. "It's the law. Any stays of two or

more days you are required by California law to do some yoga and at least one therapy session."

Marvin laughed.

"I just wanted to thank you for what you did," he said. He dropped an envelope on my desk. "That's the final payment."

"I'm just glad I could help," I said. "How is Arnella doing?"

The story had gotten a lot of press, obviously. A prominent judge and lawyer dead from a murder suicide. But so far, Kierra's involvement had been minimal as far as the reporting was concerned.

"She's doing fine," Marvin said. "At first she was worried about what people might say and do. But I think she's in a good place. We've all accepted what the situation is and we love our daughter. We would do anything for her, including helping to figure out how we can help her financially with her transition."

He took a sip of his coffee. "But we're all going to work together and make it happen. We want her to be happy. And being happy requires being true to yourself."

I nodded and Marvin got to his feet. He stuck out his hand and I shook it.

"If there's anything else I can ever do, just let me know," I said.

Marvin smiled, patted me on the shoulder and left my office.

Just then, my phone buzzed in my pocket.

I took it out and looked at the screen, saw it was Anna.

With a smile I swiped to accept the call.

"Grandmaster John speaking," I said. "How can I help you?"

THE END

AFTERWORD

Do you want more killer crime fiction, along with the chance to win free books? Then sign up for the:
DAN AMES BOOK CLUB:

Go to AuthorDanAmes.com

ALSO BY DAN AMES

DEAD WOOD

HARD ROCK

COLD JADE

LONG SHOT

EASY PREY

BODY BLOW

THE KILLING LEAGUE

THE MURDER STORE

FINDERS KILLERS

DEATH BY SARCASM

MURDER WITH SARCASTIC INTENT

GROSS SARCASTIC HOMICIDE

THE CIRCUIT RIDER

KILLER'S DRAW

SOULS OF THE DEAD

THE RECRUITER

KILLING THE RAT

BEER MONEY

TO FIND A MOUNTAIN

HEAD SHOT

DR. SLICK

CHOKE

ABOUT THE AUTHOR

Dan Ames is an international bestselling author and winner of the Independent Book Award for Crime Fiction.

www.authordanames.com
dan@authordanames.com

56513402R00119

Made in the USA
Columbia, SC
26 April 2019